Joseph Cady
New York
1984

PENGUIN BOOKS

NOTES FROM A CHILD OF PARADISE

Alfred Corn was born in Georgia in 1943. He received his B.A. from Emory University and did graduate work in French literature at Columbia. In 1967 he went to Paris as a Fulbright Fellow. He taught French briefly at Columbia and since then has made his living as a writer and teacher of creative writing. He has received many prizes and fellowships, most recently a special award from the American Academy and Institute of Arts and Letters. He lives in New York, teaching in the graduate writing programs of Columbia and the City University of New York, and spends his summers at his house in Vermont.

NOTES

FROM A

CHILD

OF

PARADISE

———

ALFRED CORN

PENGUIN BOOKS

Penguin Books Ltd, Harmondsworth,
Middlesex, England
Penguin Books, 40 West 23rd Street,
New York, New York 10010, U.S.A.
Penguin Books Australia Ltd, Ringwood,
Victoria, Australia
Penguin Books Canada Limited, 2801 John Street,
Markham, Ontario, Canada L3R 1B4
Penguin Books (N.Z.) Ltd, 182–190 Wairau Road,
Auckland 10, New Zealand

First published in the United States of America
in simultaneous hardcover and paperback editions by
The Viking Press and Penguin Books 1984

Printed in the United States of America by
Haddon Craftsmen, Scranton, Pennsylvania
Set in CRT Electra
Designed by Ann Gold

Grateful acknowledgment is made to the Maclen Music, Inc.,
for permission to reprint a selection from the song
"Within You Without You," by George Harrison. Copyright
© Northern Songs Ltd., 1967. Used by permission of
Maclen Music, Inc., c/o ATV Music Corp. All rights
reserved.

Dear Annie,

At last your letter, which I'd been wishing for.
You and Peter sound chryselephantine—
Good. Again, I'm sorry not to've managed
To get up there before you left Northampton.
        Here's the book I meant to bring; I'd rather,
Though, you had it now, there in South England's
Green and pleasant land, the setting for
Some of the poems. Will they like going back?
        Meanwhile, another question, or request:
I have a new poem (book-length) in mind.
How pleased I'd be to know, before I started,
Some distant day the dedication page
Would show your name as its friendly patron.
All Roads at Once did—may I have that honor
A second time? Which I would strive to merit.
        You're wondering why. Well, much of it should be
Devoted to the time we spent together
(Friends, lovers, then married)—an era now
Beginning to feel like ancient history.
Let's see, it's roughly a decade since we went
Our ways. (And look, we still keep close touch.)
Italy, France, New York, the Great Northwest—
That was covering quite a lot of ground.
        I know you'll have a different version of
What happened. Whom we love we're bound to mis-
Interpret, no? (A past delirium's speaking.)
Foolish to hope for full agreement now,
So vehement were our differences
Back then. Or does it go the other way?
At all events, be sure I recognize
The finely tuned responsibility
That comes with this—I mean, if you should wave
Me on with blessings. Nothing less than good
Sense, tact, fairness and humor, orders too
Large for any lower than the angels. . . .

And yet, if other vistas rose to frame
The incautious, starbright novel of our life
As sharers in a love whose icon I
Call on now for fire and sustenance
To renew those essences you first made quick
For me, breathtaking some of them, all lively—
You, a partner no more Beatrice
Carved in wax than I'm a Tuscan exile
Who never touched his Muse. . . . And please forgive
The tone of urgency that's crept in here.
I wish there'd been more news, descriptions, jokes;
And promise to do better soon. Till then,

                 Love always,

So is there no fact, no event, in our private history, which shall not, sooner or later, lose its adhesive, inert form, and astonish us by soaring from our body into the empyrean.

—EMERSON,
   "The American Scholar"

ONE

I.   In the middle of everything a voice
From the depths of the house sings out for me
To pick up the phone. Good news? New work-sheets
Watch the interrupted reader raptly
Dreaming on them start wide awake and leave
The bedroom-study (inset here one bright
Window on April 15, deep blue skies,
Branches, flowers of the cornelian
Cherry, a yard glazed with mud; and any
Number of thoughtlike, all-changeable clouds).

At the desk again, a curling snapshot
Of you, leaning against the spine of my
Old Grandgent *Commedia* makes me want
To dub under it the laughter-silvered
Tones that just now firmed up plans to visit. . . .
Ash and pearl, a seabeach in the Northwest;
Your trim sylphide body five years younger,
And calm dry gaze at least five older than
The 24 of then. . . . Heartbeat, answer:
Must part of us always remain intact?

Wind-tossed clouds, shaking branches, black spring mud,
Take up the note, new anachronisms
For the lighthearted pair, courtly beneath
Technologies, garlands of ice and fire,
Their stories indisseverably wound
Around transport in an age of airships—
So that the first vehicles gliding down
From heaven to this field where I coax home
Figures for love's arriving stars and tears,
Its scalds and wordlessnesses, are airborne.

II.   The balancing wings of hendiadys
       Shuttle me back to 1964,
       When, anticipating Dante's, that's right,
       *Hepta*centennial, a special course,
       Dark Wood to Rose of Fire in one quick spring,
       Enthralled this receptive language major;
       Who, having Time-spanned earlyward a week
       Of centuries, vacation come, would next
       Branch out in Space—a first, short trip abroad.
       So: Kennedy Air France flight lounge. *And there*

       You were. . . . What must a young woman—tawny,
       Silk-straight, Beatnik-style hair free-flowing far
       Down the back; wrapped in a Bogart trenchcoat;
       A Camel in the left hand, Gore Vidal's
       Julian in the fine right; brown eyes well up
       To Provençal standard (say, Peire Vidal's)—
       Have thought of our weedy assembly, some
       Fifty loafer types, all in a summer
       Program of French studies (language practice
       Among the papal stones of Avignon)?

       No need to guess. This much I know: right then,
       Even before takeoff, the foreshortened
       Transatlantic arc toward dawn, and that long
       Paris-to-Midi-*Mistral* trainride, when
       Our startled eyes met and glanced off, glanced, met
       Through jokes traded at all the world's expense
       (Excepting the suave, francophone elect),
       Before our timed-to-the-second *descente*
       To find our summer hosts (the French rail lines
       Are notably not late)—I'd fallen hard.

4

III.   That secret, though, played Papageno-With-
       Buttoned-Lip. There was, I gathered, someone
       Else, a fact to surprise no escort who
       Had dwelt the length of a held breath on those
       Features, or that voice between grave and gay. . . .
       And if I, for my part, had just come out
       From under six months of scarifying
       Lovesickness (smiles, hugs, promises—he was
       What I didn't then want to call a tease),
       The case seemed to have escaped your notice.

       Among your friends were men with men friends, but—
       Somehow you didn't see *me* in that light.
       Too mooncalfish, was I, hanging on your
       Least word and gesture; too understanding
       When dissatisfaction with his letters
       Showed through? Could be. I never presumed, just
       Studied to please, played whatever cards of
       Comedy and book lore I could muster.
       Lessons in love are poetry, who doubts?
       The Muse turns down uneducated louts.

       Nightly the autodidact crammed till three.
       Some more Italian (which you crisply spoke);
       The sinuous *dizains* of Scève's *Délie*;
       Arcadia (for the Countess of Pembroke)—
       Now which of us fell for the pains I took?
       Pure bliss beside the Fountain of Vaucluse,
       Recycling figures Petrarch used to use:
       Her golden-arrowed eyes, O frost that burns. . . .
       Great Freud! Since you teach men self-disabuse:
       Who makes us house our loves in Grecian urns?

IV.   Hermetic mysteries yield as I think
Of your Western side, who grew up—*golden*—
A mist-edged walk from Pacific sunsets:
Cabrillo Street in mild San Francisco. . . .
Then, those intellectually behaved teens
In Portland, Ore.; long summers at Seaside;
Yearly excursions to Ashland's outdoor
Shakespeare Theater. "American Scenes,"
These album shots (fixed to the page by four
Black chevrons, fledged compass points for travel

Out of the here-and-now) help make the shift
To a second, harmonizing subject,
This one taken from U.S history.
The double-take springing out of jumpcut
Narration can serve here to represent
What I felt when, some months back, I stumbled
Across an old childhood favorite, now
Second or third hand, in the Salvation
Army Bookstore. Title: *Westward the Course*—
Lewis and Clark's Northwest Expedition.

Reasons to claim the dusty find; or why
I spirited my book straight home, devoured
A bare account of characters distant
From the 1980s as unreserved
Patriots are likely to be—guesses? °
The fable, yes; but there are better ones.
Nostalgia? But no one really thinks of
Resetting the clock to olden days. Then?
Oracular, the Selectric taps out:
Always to have a reason is insane.

V. (History: infernally knotty yarn
    To dream into the text of a poem.
    Why not just rise, fling back the head and chant?
    It is tempting—have a go later? But,
    First, I have a story that must be told;
    At least, the striking parts, that tell themselves.
    And all the rest, I leave in trust to those
    Who know or will track down essential facts
    And dates—the "Emersonian" 1803,
    To start with; then all that comes afterward.)

    Images hovering around this subject
    Fairly elude the net of words. (Besides,
    Some who have tired of descriptive labels
    May judge that the Instamatic has earned
    Its vacation.) To stand in for them here
    Use memories or imagined vistas:
    The Rocky Mountains, Yellowstone—landscapes
    Our 19th-century Cosmoramic
    Painters raised to a visionary, plane
    Representation of America. . . .

    Once home, I skimmed my "juvenile" straight through.
    I read myself upriver—did I doze . . . ?
    Mighty Adonic, Father of Waters,
    Now pour them Lethe as the course runs true.
    Au revoir, New Orleans! the bold forgetters
    Will barter steeples for Montana snows;
    Collect their samples—flora, fauna, crew—
    The Bird Woman, Sacajawea, knows!
    The bright-plumed local, child of what they spanned,
    Interprets whom she guides—through Promised Land.

VI. Promised? To, and by the empire builders.
Native Americans raised on tribal
Wars that kept them in Malthusian trim
Can never have understood the import
Of European territorial
Practices: surveys, claims staked, conquests, deeds
Drawn up on living paper, signed in blood.
Followers of that history must numb
To atrocity, tableaux no Bierstadt
Ever quite undertook—the murder of

Earlier human possibilities.
When cultures meet they first exchange a style
Of killing; and what is to choose between,
On one hand, mechanical massacre
By firearms, and then maximum-suffering
Rape and dismemberment on the other.
It takes a gross genre like Western film
To confront the bloodbaths, so many slain
Under the wide sky, where black wingspans wheel
And drop to feed in dust-devil stillness. . . .

Westward the Course sidestepped the hard topic
For so did national consciousness, start to
Finish—at least until a war ago.
In this as in so many other ways,
You were (for one slightly in arrears) our
Timeghost's vessel. That Beat garb and lingo
(Once recivilized, I'd know it as "hip")
Went deeper than, say, the latest Naked
Poem. There was real news from N.Y.U.;
And I . . . had nothing to lose but my chains.

VII.　Politics, Art, and Pleasure love a guide;
　　　So that, if afternoons would find us side
　　　By side and toiling up a cobbled street—
　　　Nondescript and bohémienne—no treat
　　　Could equal our Platonic dialogues.
　　　Peripatetic but on shapely legs,
　　　In espadrilles you tramped the rightist down,
　　　The macho (Christ, what dolts), the puritan.
　　　I listened. Bright glints dangled from your ears;
　　　So delicate; but (*pang*) the lobes were pierced.

　　　Mind aims for summits, spurred on by debate,
　　　Or settles for the Garden of the Popes
　　　Beside the palace, over rocky slopes
　　　And chalky banks Rhone waters bathe. The great
　　　Bridge, with its Romanesque chapelle—now *there*
　　　Dance and Provençal song and sunburnt mirth
　　　Would find their proper stage. (For what it's worth,
　　　On the dry bed *under* the bridge is where
　　　They danced.) You stretched, exhaling caporal.
　　　Blue atmospheres: *Gitane qui fume au bal.*

　　　Day after bonedust day, July unwinds.
　　　At morning class our Valéry rests while
　　　For a brief spell M. Brombert reminds
　　　Us all (who haven't read it) that the style
　　　Of *Roland Furieux* as well includes
　　　The serious and the broad—he could recite,
　　　In fine Italian, some octaves rimés:
　　　"La luce candida. . . ." (A desk away
　　　A Dartmouth fullback's doodling busty nudes.
　　　You glance at me. Eyes flash. The candid light.)

VIII.	Olivetree and vineyard; red dust; wild thyme;
Wind-ruffled hectares of grassy wheat, flecked
With carmine poppies; square stonework tower
And barrel vault cowled in tiles of a church
Keeping watch in the fields till one bright star
Struck the angelus. . . . We crossed and recrossed
The lands between Nîmes, Aix, Les Baux, then
Down to Aigues Mortes and Sète to stand before,
Sacred name, the Mediterranean.
Some places ask us to live up to *them*.

Wherefore, if we wandered through Arles to find
The Aliscamps (I, too, had to stop and
Look it up, that Roman graveyard Dante
Plucked from his memory to help render
The sarcophagi or large fish-poachers
He simmered his Christian heretics in,
Lids ajar from the steamhead of dissent);
Or if we crept tentative steps over
The Pont du Gard; or strained to catch the gist
Of *Le Soulier de satin* (drama of

A New World explored, passions, storms, shipwrecks)
At Orange's antique colosseum;
Or downed our stinging Bastille Day *pastis*
At metal café tables camouflaged
In shadow leaves from plane trees overhead—
Every warrant promised time grew mythic
For those who met eternal things halfway:
First, by supposing them; then taking steps
To find a likeminded soul; and last, the . . .
Arena where the myth you shared might shine.

IX. Doctrinal variants on Western Civ:
Marxism-Leninism, "l'art pour l'art";
A faith in Jung or Christian Science, naïve
Materialism—Pope was right, to err
Et cetera. If some would charge, say, Scève
With lifting Dante's old New Style, a mere
Pointed mention of Guinizelli, of,
Well, Virgil, Plato, Homer (overkill)
Should clear him. Who plays fair in war and love?
In art, revision was traditional.

Americans have changed all that, that is,
Each new begetter shoots for first and all
Begin anew: "Now circle round—" (crowd noise).
It leaves me reeling. Enough class. (Our term
Has ended. Travels will sunder. Frowns, sighs.
But wills and plans are—Casablanca—firm.)
I did detect, though, some reluctance on
Your part to join your . . . friend. His name was Norm?
No, Bert. Malicious rhymes were roiling in
My brain. "You'll write? American Express

In Florence." "Oh, Al, sure I will. What fun!
You're off to Florence, aren't you lucky!" (Kiss.)
Then, told your four-week jaunt in—Germany?—
Was courtesy his Yamaha, I guess
I blanched or something. (Laugh smile talk. But—why?)
"He's there already," weakly you explained.
"I said I'd go, I promised. Too late now."
Across the Rhone a bloody sun declined
To hollow thumping in my chest. "I know,
But, I think I'm—." (Closeup.) You rose, fled, and—

X.   And in a matter of days you and he
Were plying the Romantische Strasse
As I, creaky-eyed from a sleepless night
On the Geneva rapido, stepped from
Its destination into the Tuscan
Dawn. A shaft of sun struck the marble spire
Of Santa Maria Novella. Trucks
Dodged and tromboned warnings at the addled
Wayfarer, who lurched into their path, borne
Up on awe, his ballast a duffelbag.

—Till it should be dumped at the first hostel
To unbolt gray doors before a yawning
Porter. From the taps of the cracked basin
In my room the new *acqua* filled my palms
To splash away fatigue and third-class grime.
Twenty is ceaseless, so in nothing flat
Its feet were bounding down the spiral stairs.
Already you were being written to,
For instinctively I saw it took two
To make the monumental visible.

Proxy recording angel, were you not
My cicerone, wafting me to site
On glorious site—the Campanile, got
Up as a wedding-cake; the Duomo's light-
As-air stoneribboned mitre; or the grave
Oneirism of Michelangelo's *Night?*
That birdwarm Giotto fresco in the nave
Of Santa Croce? Or this—but your eyes
Are weary, since they're mine. The rest we'll save.
Domani, at the Gates of Paradise.

XI. But, first, earlier matters want to be
Brought forward—and preferably on board
The Experiment, where some "Volunteers
Of the Discovery of the West" make
Their struggled-for knots up the Missouri
Beyond St. Louis. William Clark, who termed
The expedition "an undertaking
Of difficult and parlous nature," turns
To his co-captain, his friend (I see him
Standing quietly near the tiller), and asks,

What final outcome can be expected?
No answer from the olive-gray waters
Where huge driftwood treestumps thrust up bleached roots
That claw and find no purchase in silent
Air, futurity but the lightest breeze
That blows from the low green shore. Kentucky
And Virginia will have sent out their sons
To write this new chapter in a story
Long since venerable, the exploration
Of fields lying farther to the golden

West, the abstract place, notions for which all
The half-formed Elysian mythscapes dreamed
In Europe's longing for Arcadia
Supplied—so much at odds with the extremes
Of climate, rough profusion of nature,
And resistance to invasion from those
Who since prehistory had wrested bare
Livelihoods from inhospitable lands,
The rocks, the trees, the tangled green syntax
Of the North American wilderness.

XII.　For America is the Garden of
　　　Paradox: new golden land, it was brave
　　　And new to them; but in itself, old, old
　　　As only sheer geology can be,
　　　Before history comes to give some scale
　　　To the monotone of eternity,
　　　Overlaying a grid of date and place,
　　　Memorable wars, claims and boundaries
　　　That would supplant the concrete calendar
　　　Of aborigines whose clock was myth.

　　　Wilderness and garden, where liberty
　　　Flourished, dishevelment of death mingled
　　　With life renewed, the green seedling rooted
　　　In crumbling brown peat from its fallen great
　　　Parent, that brought down also the cordage
　　　Of wild grape, not in defeat but patience;
　　　The tendril's springy drill, the classic leaf
　　　Seize and cling to the rise of each new tree,
　　　Sharers with them all in light sought upward—
　　　Pillars of a temple; a roof of crowns.

　　　When one has left his house and village green,
　　　Society of women, customs, law,
　　　The handworked coverlet and mantel chime,
　　　Roof in imbricate shingles, silver smoke,
　　　With stick and pouch, a polished rifle, he
　　　Makes his solitary way through forests;
　　　Then, well along, in a birch-lined clearing,
　　　He pauses for the vista—the lost trail
　　　Back, the uphill climb to summits far off
　　　In azure-white noon—and feels an old fear.

XIII.	*The Cenozoic continent, roughwork*
	Of earthquake and volcanic fire, relic
	Of the long glacial night, an enemy
	To civil settlement, keeps to its place
	In alien majesty above the towns.
	Habitation and tillage have never
	Sunk deep enough into the land; forests
	Echoing the patient blows of axes
	Send out a wide emptiness on the edge
	Of the faint cicada trill as night falls.

	You gazing at the hillside brook will breathe
	In its white ruffles the fragrance of lost
	February snows, mountains men seldom
	Visit, if at all. And leave where they are
	Trillium and ladyslipper, that languish
	In gardens, happiest far from people's
	Tending: the dark wood whispers, Do not stay.
	Turning back to houses is renewing
	The will to construct a human dwelling,
	Yourself inasmuch as not of Nature. . . .

	All savage creatures must then be redeemed;
	And fought down the black swell, the echoed void.
	The voice crying out in the wilderness
	Is a civil war, for deep within lies
	A darker wilderness, fear of Nature,
	Sacrifice of self, where the wound bleeds word.
	Sinners in the Hands of an Angry God,
	Wring a psalm from the forestries of Hell,
	A knot garden of Miltonic baroque—
	MAGNALIA on the Vine of the Lord.

XIV.   No letters? The clerk gave a pitying
        Italianate shake of the head as I
        Turned, slunk back, pushed open wheeling glass doors
        That broke in pieces gold bars of morning
        Light, refracted javelins hurled through crowds
        Thronging the dim arcades. *Stop choking. Time*
        To wake up, forget her. A third person
        Had thrust into the deepest of my dream—
        Damn, even fools tire of playing the fool.
        This one had red blood, was twenty, hungry.

        A long hour in the subaqueous glow
        Of the throne room or swim tank that housed
        Young *David*, celestially gymnastic—
        Copies in plaster of whom still preside
        Over a million knickknack collections
        In the free world, our first teenage idol.
        His outsize hand lolled in all innocence
        Against the lean flank, like a slingshot just
        Having let fly its missile to the brow.
        Lodged there, this opened a piercing third eye.

        Which now would help one see the city plain?
        Humanist Contra Naturam, a speech
        Cognate with city life, must sometimes reach
        New heights where sacred aims appear profane.
        The probing mind fixed on the patterned stones
        Of a square crossed, or breaking free to stare
        At Babel building far, or nightspot near—
        The clientèle lilting in foreign tones
        And offering friendly help for what disturbs—
        Began to practice Second Nature's verbs.

XV.　To take that step, to love whatever asks
　　　A boldness or nerve much like pure folly
　　　Since hearts can crack long before the obit.
　　　When Freud develops his Leonardo,
　　　He wants to show how passion fled into
　　　A lust for knowledge: research as foreplay,
　　　Findings, an orgasm of certitude.
　　　Posterity got those calm bronze matrons,
　　　Some sketches for the biplane *Icarus*,
　　　And the symphonic thought of his Notebooks.

　　　And as for Leonardo? A reined-in
　　　Liking for handsome faces and trouble
　　　Coaxing any painting to completion—
　　　A patient history supplied for Freud's
　　　Dantesque mythology of the psyche.
　　　Leonardo was "Everyartist"; and
　　　Civilization must be discontent.
　　　True, though one day ecstasy might be ours,
　　　Sweeter perhaps for having been delayed:
　　　The scale to Heaven plays a flight of stairs. . . .

　　　Think of Brunetto Latini, figure
　　　That few dwellers in the City of Dis
　　　Equaled, his shade to Dante resembling
　　　A stripped-down runner in the Verona
　　　Heat; and more like *"quelli che vince, non
　　　Colui che perde."* Eternity meant
　　　Entering the race of the archetypes?
　　　A contest in behalf of life that might
　　　Cost one's own. (*Vulture stabs at the liver;
　　　Heart's treasure is safe, up beyond the stars.*)

XVI. Bellissima Roma laminata:
       Among so many Eternal buried,
       Which City will the latest pilgrim seek?
       Given the nil viaticum to hand,
       A shaken but exhilarated leaf
       Let go from the *Tuscan Oak*, then fallen
       And fairly stuck on pavement travertine,
       Communist Rome was what I noticed most
       Rumbling through my walls (ALBERGO CIPPO),
       A long walk south of Nero's golden house.

       The blood-red seas parted, all centuries
       Laid open to the investigator,
       Unscathed somehow, though he prowled monuments
       Even Horace left in less ruined state.
       Nerva to Boniface and Il Duce:
       Human gore rose transformed by alchemy
       Into a serial glory dazzling
       Every witness . . . who lived to sell the tale.
       Yes, but the sun would set. I'd find myself
       A dinner, Piazza della Quercia:

       Mounds of pasta, sauced mud-red. *Close your eyes.*
       Don't think. Down the hatch. . . . The perfumed Roman
       Night, night that was a somnambulism
       Through marble grottoes, searippled with—*light*:
       Rakes and jets of light spending prodigal,
       Diamond acupuncture, O starstrung harp. . . .
       Which by dawn had stopped playing, in rose-gray
       Stillness—. To start to climb the Spanish Steps
       Meant fusing with a ragtag band of us,
       The gathering new wave of the Sixties.

18

XVII.   Every resource dries up at last, no doubt
Even the italic font. All aboard
While I still have third-class fare—express to
Paris! (Our study group will reconvene
Two days hence, the Quartier where also, once,
Latin instead of franglais was spoken.)
"Ciao," to my cohorts, whose polyglot names
Begin to slip from memory just as
The train pulls out from Termini. . . . Later,
Slumped in the corridor as we tunneled

Toward France, forlorn farmwives with trussed capons
Jostling on either side (this was far from
Any "breezing on trust funds through the world"),
I mulled and mused. Would you be waiting there
(I'd still had no word) on the rue St. Jacques?
Or would our holidays have altered us
Beyond recognition? This time I must
Try to keep cool and not turn back into
That one-way street—first with him, then with you.
(Just which "persuasion" was I, anyhow?)

—Achoo! What—? Chicken feather. Where am I?
Train on the way to Paris. Switching track.
Not much light yet. Dying of thirst. Why, why
Did—ouch. Whose foot's—mine. Oh my aching back. . . .
Hélène   vous avez quitté Florence
Rayonnant   lueurs célestes   vos yeux
Versent comme jadis leurs suaves feux
O Beauté   soumis à telle Romance
Simple berger   à l'univers je dis
"Hélène est divine selon Pâris."

XVIII.   Paris. City where *le Mal*, reclining
In the mufti of ennui, sighs and thrives;
Where an Angel named Change spins a silver-
Spiraling arc across one's zinc-gray days;
And discourse will be new, or not at all.
(I must defer, though, for a while the signs
Of his brilliance, this Prince of Capitals;
But I promise now, as I swore back then,
"Je reviendrai"; nor let this one-shot life
Be lived without some pages from his book.)

I scanned the faces of our weathered crew:
You nowhere among them. A statue named
Crestfallen, there I stood till rumor buzzed
You were still en route, a day or two late.
Traffic symphony: the trumpets sounded,
Renault, Peugeot, O seasons and castles,
Azay-le-Rideau! Off to the Louvre;
Or Notre Dame, to light a votive—no,
Not quite. But a kaleidoscopic rose
(Stone lace, stained light) should help me pass the hours

Until you came. . . . Then that blue dusk might hide
As well stricken glances when I brought you
There with me again. Alas, brought you both;
For he had followed. Casual, shaggy,
A profile drawn from the Jerusalem
Of the Kings (in fact, a kid from Brooklyn),
No way despicable, what could I say
To him? Goodbye. To you also. Goodbye.
(The plane rose, leaving that New World.) But *not*
Resigned. . . . Staked claim! I'd see you made good yet.

XIX.   "Now I am one-and-twenty," so I heard
        Myself think. Too hectic to take a bow
        When in Rome the day had come to confer
        Its ghostly toga on me, here was time
        To ponder a civic status needing
        Two Augusts more to seem at all confirmed.
        Back to home and country. And to a last
        Year of school, which, though senior-level, felt
        Retarded, the mid-Atlantic limbo
        Rushed to agree with him who rode it out.

        Now, with just twice his span of consciousness
        Under my hat, should I envy, pity,
        Mock that fledgling life? No more, I guess, than
        Any other other person's. The bulk
        Of his archive has been settled on me;
        And sift as I will its strange content keeps
        A far-gone quality I recognize
        Yet would no sooner try to reassume
        Than squeeze into the vintage jeans he wore,
        Or reread his latest favorite book.

        Now, I know, will have been that misnomer
        That rarely holds the fort for long—so brief
        A stay it couldn't always accustom
        Its golden hoard of clairvoyance to all
        We might have meant to one another. See
        How slowly we move to be reconciled;
        How stoutly jetstream contention baffles;
        How reluctantly we touch ground, even
        In the tall city where, back then, I could
        Visit—believing or not—*The World's Fair.*

XX. Relationships. Expand the repertoire,
Equality and fairness the high goal.
Already launched, this warm subversion meant
To break the Fifties' hierarchical
Chain of public strictures, arid stoppage,
In favor of a freshening Ich-und-Du.
We had our reasons and our precedents.
If till now humane friendships between men
And women seldom flourished, still you and
I, exchanging letters, confidences,

Places, almost, in revelations fierce
As personal, it seemed likely, might clear
A truer way of being together.
Also, for us, epistolary breadth,
The *illusion* of presence touched springs deep
With inwardness, that never would have welled
Had we fallen in step with the prescribed
Ritual. . . . A year of letters, each scribbled,
Rash intensity. Why you'd stopped seeing
Him. Who looked tempting, or who bright these days.

And, what about me? Had I found someone—?
The Tom-and-Dick names calmly, with risqué
Charm, stamped Approved. Then, a corresponding
Regret: that you would have to abandon,
You supposed, the attraction felt for—me!
(Girls talked that way? *You* did. Uncouth to be
Taken aback.) A red flush rose and burned,
Ballpoint racing to reply, *Everything
Is possible if* . . . But you were far
Away. When, where, could we see each other?

XXI. Just under halfway on, a decade stands
      Out as itself; gets hawked from the newsstands;
      Then scores in deeper; and pockets the dice.
      (Already we'd seen a president fall,
      Killed by random madness.) Then, late that fall,
      Rumblings from California; for you
      Had gone back West, "the Berkeley transfer." Like
      Our generation's Best Minds used to like
      To say, the San Francisco scene was what
      Was happening, for life and style alike.

      I still don't quite imagine you out there.
      The Terrace. Marx-tinted glasses. And there
      Was, you wrote, a paved walk jammed with tables—
      Leaflets, manifestoes, world-seen-red. Plus
      An antic Harpo-Groucho fringe A-plus
      Students like you smiled at as you passed.
      Politics mattered. Sex and pop-songs too:
      "We are the LPs that we listen to."
      In residence were Ginsberg and Baez,
      Setting things up—to mention only two.

      Yes, but Leary'd dropped in (or out) and joined
      Forces with heads for whom a decent joint,
      Once, had been enough. (Capsule sacrament,
      A.k.a. LSD, I'm afraid
      We mostly bought your propaganda: "Frayed
      Electric Chord, Illumination, turn
      Us on!" Legally, by U.S. Mail, came
      A trip from you. Taken. . . . *Then time oncame*
      A skewed movie   hot crestrisen rainbow
      Sirenbeam   Homing in the dreamers came   )

XXII.　Yet come so far, and junk it all, one's class,
Degree, life plan? That time we both refused.
No B.A. candidates were ever more
Impassioned by their subject nor less crass
About its value. French génie: amused
And metaphysical, keen wit no bore
Survived a reading of intact—Racine,
Baudelaire, and Valéry, are you still heard?
When reason marries fire and verses mean
Their timbres, *Alchimistes* transcribe the Word.

Yes, most of all, faun-eared Rimbaud, the clown,
The demon-angel of a twilit age.
The old ideas wondered where to shoot?
"Sighting the topmost peaks, one first aims down,
Inferno just that dive *Là-Bas*. Come rage
Against the stolid millions, horn and flute;
Practice whatever pleases you, and learn,
Delirious, the wisdom of the mad."
With him as guide, could later adepts turn—
Well, evil, no; but might drum up some bad.

And if his days were short they only prove
The gods abducted him to their own climes,
Where no one mocked the seer, nor gave the lie
To sibyls speaking from the sacred grove,
Or told the Muse to read the daily *Times*.
—Not that one didn't keep abreast, or try
To designate all clods and prudes passé. . . .
Aimais-je un rêve? A visionary gleam.
Insomnia, I knew; and how to say,
"This dreamer wakes no dreamer from the Dream."

XXIII.   *Des Peaux-Rouges criards les avaient pris*
Pour cibles. . . . Amerindians, their stock
Proliferating from the Bering Strait
To Tierra del Fuego; interpreted
As every man the colonizers thought
To find in Nature's Paradise or Hell.
Among disruptive agents, consider
The plague of ill-fitting mythography;
And the brackish mouthful of fraud tasted
By those who took baptism at its word.

Doña Marina and Pocahontas—
If they'd known where collaboration led. . . .
And you, Sacajawea, Shoshone,
An island soul uprooted from your tribe,
Lacking a context with Sioux and Mandan,
Wife to a trapper, his eyes in your child's—
The expedition must have seemed a wind
That force and drift of chance had meant to raise—
Force that flickering lesson learned by firelight,
Fumes, seared meat, coals. . . . And resignation.

I like to see you in a younger guise,
The face less like an eagle's, nor the gaze
Sibylline, a sculptural armature
Of bone upholding at cheek and forehead
The unfathomable fable it half
Wanted to tell. Before blunt happenstance
Had come to lock in place your figurehead
At the sharp prow of *The Experiment*,
Breasting river waters, patient, splintered,
Your eyes forever open, bright with fear.

XXIV. With the dawn of the Aquarian Age
        (Peacepipes, buckskin, beads, Apache headbands,
        Warpaint, and communal lodging), comment
        Tried out the decal New Tribalism—
        No more superficial than the others,
        "Pinko-Communist" or "Flower Children,"
        Affixed to the brash under-30 crowds;
        Anyone could see, from the beginning,
        That atavisms of many colors
        Waved us on with bold, primeval standards.

        Now where was I? Well, working hard to catch
        Up with the vanguard; and with your cheerful
        Incitements making some modest headway.
        Meanwhile the storm began to aggravate.
        Loud demonstrations, a new Movement for
        Free Speech. Your tersely scribbled bulletin:
        "Sproul Hall taken over . . . hauled up by rope
        Sling to the second story . . . a noisy
        Night on bare tiles, with the hard-core leftists . . .
        Hip-hurrays, dialectic, and plotting."

        What's more, the insurgent charismatic,
        Mario—call him Savonarola—
        Was forcibly escorted from the Greek
        Amphitheater, where an indignant
        But exhilarated assembly found
        The Administration guilty as charged.
        Further strikes. Arrests. Concessions. At last,
        Bay Area skies cleared. Sunshine shone.
        (In politics, the Californian
        Is radical? Conservative? Is both.)

XXV.   The schools were roughly equal; if I chose
       Columbia, New York had tipped the scale.
       Pleasures of Cambridge, of New Haven, for
       Now be left to the imagination. . . .
       Naïve bravado signed the dotted line,
       Closed the envelope. Sealed, stamped, and mailed it—
       Awareness growing how documents mount
       Up and up until one day they assume
       Our own name. (The stack's tall enough by now
       So they bear out the claim? Question tabled

       While I put in précis my last summer
       Back home.) Deep South. Georgia that spills over
       Into Florida, same dew, same green shade.
       Yet day by day it felt less familiar,
       The liveoaks streaming gray beards of moss; noon
       As a whitehot arclight; and outside town,
       Beyond the newest, farthest shopping mall,
       Broad fields of tobacco and gleaming corn.
       UNEEDA BISCUIT, CLABBER GIRL—the white
       Church of God marked each ten-mile interval.

       Who'd seen Paris, this no longer suited;
       No more than age twelve's perfect obedience.
       July heat. A firewrought salvo of words.
       I packed a bag, drove to a rooming house
       Across the tracks, and made it my castle—
       The naked lightbulb swinging on its cord,
       Lino floors, threadbare chenille, swaybacked bed.
       I smoked, read *The Unvanquished*, slept, and dreamed.
       Within two weeks, explanations, pardons.
       The prodigal returned—to say goodbye.

XXVI.   One of me is braving the crowds right now,
Under the dome of Grand or Penn Station,
New blood pumped into the Metropolis
From the heartland—unless that archetype
Balzac perfected and Dreiser retooled
Has run out of steam, as sounds unlikely.
Awkward, forward, ill-dressed, head-in-the-clouds,
The child of the provinces hardly waits
A week before unloading what he *knows*
His last illusion is; and buys new clothes.

Tall ectomorph, in less than a month I
Had shrunk to gaunt on low-budget dinners,
Calories spent on tickets—theater,
Ballet; though spectacles more dumbfounding
Still cost but the time it took to appraise
A thunderous street scene of skyscrapers,
Wheels, and heterodox pedestrians.
Lost souls all—including the observer?
I stared at glassfaced buildings; they stared back.
A broker bowed into a Cadillac.

The first subway strike kept a splenetic
Traffic snarl awake and roaring all night,
A pedal-point for Thought's tireless urbane
Experiment. *What to do, how to love,*
One asked; then fired some shots into the dark. . . .
A former self grabs the mike to sigh, "How
Bored and lonely we are." That overcoat,
Representative destiny let in,
I found, too many blasts of razor cold.
Sore throat, fever, congestion, chills. The old

XXVII. Walls of the room in the old apartment
I rented from an ancient lady cracked
And flaked, it seemed, in the very moment
With steamheat torsions of several extra
Degrees pounded through the dim labyrinth
In my skull and the racked radiators.
On the hour I dosed myself with cognac
From the flamethrower flask looming nearby.
Mrs. Smith appeared. Rather, twin gold-rimmed
Lenses on a whitehaired crone doll untrimmed

Their fever wicks as she crept in to ask,
"Influenza? My husband died of that,
End of the War. He looked a lot like you."
The door closed on what ought to be panic
On my part; except that I am elsewhere,
Reliving what will have been happening
These last months in the blackout underground,
Knocking at peepholed doors; which would open.
I thought of you, a continent away.
Who was I? Would you tell me? I heard you say,

Decades inside, *Now go to sleep. I'm here.* . . .
All right. And someone sputtered out beyond
The shoals of midnight, and out past the leer
Of flashing beacons—yellow, green, and red—
The shipwrecked passengers, a wailing host.
That desert island, should I call it home?
Who could decide when everything was lost?
I reached, clung to a spar, eyes meeting yours
As dawn came up. And whispered, *Still, we might*—
Then woke. The bedside lamp relit my night.

XXVIII. New York had its positives, though—among
Them, new Jewish friends, I stopped to reflect
One silver-gray morning, feeling the verve
And mindfulness of my adopted town.
Observable as well the parentage
Of European modernism here
In this American alertness, tone,
Its searching modes of art. Intricately
Fresh styles of voice rang in my ears, a laugh
Handed down a thousand years of cities. . . .

Clear eyes, resistance to prettified, canned,
Or trumped-up consolations, does one learn
These things? Learn how to object when trammeled
By *any* rubric, praise above all? Then
To fall serious, set jaw the single
Clue to battles inside: *What's the next step*
With the best chance of keeping us alive?
I didn't ask for this. Was it too much
To expect—. If there were some good reason . . .
Appointed task: wrestling with the angel.

Unsayable harms, the shock-negative
Ineffability of suffering—
Not revisited here. Instead summon
Memories, near-sensations, instances
Of firm counsel and support; a warm, wry
Turn of thought; the lined, smiling face. Also,
The heart that weighed chances for a long time
In many lands and said, "If I am not
For myself, who will be for me? And if
I am for myself alone, who am I?"

XXIX.   Forced immobility in the winter
         Quarters at what the captains settled on
         Naming Fort Mandan made for a species
         Of leisure—to reflect, compose misspelled
         Diaries; and provision the larder
         With antelope and buffalo, butchered
         Into veal and steaks stored under the stars
         In North Dakota's minus-thirty deep
         Freeze. . . . Or, that dark November, when they massed
         At the zenith, to watch the Northern Lights.

         Invincible indifference, midnight
         As miracle: electron phalanxes
         Downswept from the Arctic as Polaris
         Summoned aloft flaring solstice searchlights
         In diamond blue, in irised green and red—
         Palisades, loom stretched with flame, a fireharp
         Baldaquino wrung into icicle
         Canticle by sharp solar wind, facets
         And panoptic discords forelightening
         Apocalypse's skywide burning glass.

         Uncanny display, majestically cold,
         Out of reach to the tiny spectators'
         Frostbite and fevers, steady threat of death—
         Will it hold up as a balanced figure
         For universal law? Alien; vast;
         So immovable responses are just
         To howl as long as the bellows will pump,
         Or bow before the unknowable dark. . . .
         Dark as why, with knowledge of what they lose,
         Men choose their own wills, their own wars and wounds.

XXX.   Millions of postwar childhoods, sunlit grass
       Lush under sparkle-brilliant lawn sprinklers,
       Green conduits snaking back through shadows
       To water-funds that would gush forever. . . .
       Sunlight for the child, once he could reason,
       Yielded to shadows; of these, two place-names
       Stand for the legacy of the World War.
       Hiroshima, which taught him that Mother
       Earth could die, with all her children. Auschwitz,
       That men could sink even below evil.

       Logical murder. The approaching end
       Of history and love. What lives could bear
       Up under those mutilations of hope;
       Or who take part in governing a world
       Still radioactively inhuman?
       Once (much too old for the game) I took off
       On a playground swing and began to glide,
       Exhilaration up and vertigo
       Down, a dazzled pendulum seesawing
       Between iceblue ecstasy and panic—.

       "We were all like that." Back and forth between
       Summer-camp prankishness and precocious
       Gravity, something odd and overdrawn,
       Surely, in both extremes. The golden mean
       Couldn't be kept, it seemed, or not for long.
       So, when Johnson began to escalate
       The War for Peace in Southeast Asia—NUKE
       THE CONG a cherished hawkshrill slogan—gay
       And solemn, our Children's Crusade was launched,
       To save America and Vietnam.

XXXI.   Giants of government and industry:
How much serious attention did we
Suppose them paying to early protests?
Barbaric flagspeak syllables babbled
On prime-time TV puffed hard to maintain
That dissent-in-any-form-is-treason,
And lovers-of-their-country-think-in-herds.
No! As we stood ready to demonstrate
On the model of battles recently
Engaged in Mississippi and Selma.

In the midst of private half-cocked confusions
And despairs, the relief in having found
A clearcut cause to espouse and fight for.
The same felt about you. Whatever else
Had been sucked into the existential
Vacuum, love at least still breathed and let shine
Its flickering pencil of flame even
In the darkest nights of Dread and Nothing.
For, if by day I thought about the war,
By night my fantasies came back in love.

Shared indignation made a bond the more.
You wouldn't stand by calmly while your male
Peers were conscripted to do the country's
Dirty work—thus the new note of concern
Underlining your words in so many
Long transcontinental conversations.
Yet war itself comes as no truce to love.
I went on waging mine. And, happy days,
Hit a winning streak. Our term breaks were near.
Would you fly here to see me? Yes? Yes! *Yes!*

XXXII.   The period of getting to know you
          Again, in flesh (no more disembodied
          Words conveyed here by air or telephone),
          Began in a taxi headed uptown:
          "Columbia—the University."
          Voluble, bodied words filled the backseat
          And spilled out the window over Broadway's
          Unspooling cinema—outspoken signs,
          Crowds bundled up, gloved, the traffic islands
          Heaped with the last-of-January's snow.

          The end is a beginning. Then, if you
          No longer were the paper-doll cutout
          Absence had fashioned, the new rounded-out
          You made me forget that pale aura'd wraith
          Conjured up on many an empty night
          Since we parted. . . . Hand in hand, up steps toward
          The domed library. Alma Mater, bronze
          And green, lifted arms streaming patina
          As if *she'd* summoned the clear skies and sun
          That just then flooded our urban snowscape.

          Other sights as backdrop for the nonstop
          Dialogue? Grant's Tomb, somehow—ah! I know,
          The Riverside Campanile—*Souvenir*
          De Florence—this time an American
          Elevator to make us all less down
          To earth. Still, the last flight one has to climb
          By manpower, even if left breathless
          And fuddled upon reaching the lookout:
          River; salt-bright ice; blue glare; vibrant snow.
          Crash! Bells strike, carillons chime SKY SUN JOY.

XXXIII.   Lamplight. The livingroom of a former
Schoolmate of yours, now turned over to us
For a night. I opposite from you, lost
In thought, holding a mug of warm mulled wine
Tight in my cold hands. From the overworked
Radiator, stretches, creaks, thuds, complaints—
About how conversation falls away
Into brittle phrases (color them tense
And pulsing with adrenaline); about
How seldom the right move suggests itself.

The furled cinnamon stick drowned in red wine;
Sentences blown off course by gusts of yawn;
Mickey Mouse pointing toward the eleventh
Hour from a toy clock on a wooden shelf.
Now or never. One gliding motion, and—
There. Soft, fragrant hair, cool peach cheek. A kiss.
Clangor of burglar alarms somewhere, then
Sirens. Your sigh: "I want you, but, I guess—
We should wait a day or two, until—. No?
Well, I certainly don't mind if you don't."

For details on that level will not daunt
Whoever has taken a life-or-death
Plunge—or will they? All the suppleness, warmth,
Curious modelings of flesh, the scent
Of cinnamon, of peat, and still no wild
Loss of consciousness. . . . A calm, cool embrace.
"Happens all the time. Not important. Let's—
Another time—again." Angelic words
Partly wasted on him who got up, dressed;
Walked back home through ice, hopes degree zero.

XXXIV. The rising mercury at dawn implied
That somewhere was a spring, and winter's night,
Shedding its heavy armor, soon would go
Breakneck away—quick, silver runnels both
Of us would take to heart as earth's new blood. . . .
Now, though, *I felt like shit, like dying.* But
You called, we talked. I let on how I was
(More than a little sheepish) sorry not
To have stayed there with you last night, and all.
"No problem. Meet for coffee? I feel raw

Myself; as though I'd let you down, or failed
To—." This I wouldn't hear of. Through a scald
Of anguish, "Wait!" I croaked. "We'll talk later."
Hung up. Got dressed. Ran out. The gunned motor
Of hope and love put muscle, spring and speed
In the long lopes that brought me to your side:
A breathless kiss, your playful eyes, your laugh.
We fumbled—so? No scars. Just shrug it off?
(Heavenly Wisdom, Woman was your name.)
The day eased by. . . . Now, back to your place? Come!

Heavenly Willingness, in human form:
A rising cumulus began to storm
The sunset battlements aglow on high
Summits of longing, where to groan or sigh
Was pleasure's selflessness that tried to speak—
And spoke in rain, in lightning flash, oblique
Zigzags of synapse, thunder, hail. You rose,
O sweet, as laughter bathed in ripples, froze
Eternity; then broke through to the far
Deep reds of love—and lo, the Evening Star.

36

TWO

I.   To run their small boat faster, these two
        Sails, tension and release in balance,
From pole to pole alive, send it scudding
Across the sea under a genial gust
Of animal spirits. . . . Silver light. Now
He wakes to ask what embodiment she
Is beside him here, smooth-shouldered, lapped
In sleep, a nimble, complementary warmth.
This time is not the same as yesterday's.
He swallows, fights the tug toward tenderness
As her eyes falter open, comprehension
Welling up, to rest on him. Lips part
In smiles, the first of many similar.
A stretch underlines them both; rustle
Of bedclothes, limbs, murmured tones, whispers. . . .

For her, expanses of feeling: contentment, salt
Certainty of having become overnight
A pair, twin names caught up in one blaze.
He's the awkwardly gentlest so far, gazing
Down in sturdy calm from a propped elbow,
Hair ruffled in contrary directions,
The coals of ardor breathed on, glowing.
Added, a bluish shading when she counts
The handful of conversations left them, a short
Week to unfurl the new dispensation. . . .
She hears silent urgings, maternal accents,
The same that last night saw to getting in
Something for breakfast; the wish to give pleasure.
Muffins, café au lait poured like tribute.
Love flares across a bowl of oranges.

II.   Airport goodbyes, a numb malaise to play
Convincingly, hum with a science-fiction
Aura; the movie they saw yesterday,
Alphaville, supplies what French inflection.
Some whispered ashen phrases beset their lips,
Amputation a pain novel, vague,
Brutal. She turns to leave, her handclasp slips
From his, and—gone. Fade. Cut. And slowly segue
To a small dim room a few weeks hence:
He folds and seals his pages, rereads hers. . . .
For lovers make of letters sacraments.
At stroke of pen alone the body stirs,
This silent rite replacing touch with sense
That undershoots the dam of wordlessness,
Expression sharply spurred on by duress.

No need, however, to assume that they
Hadn't a second thought about their chances.
He sees arresting faces in his way
On the bright avenues; and, yes, she dances
In and out of an arm or two that spring.
Mere stopgaps to outwit the interim,
For on September first—let freedom ring!
She'll fly to N.Y.C. to live with him.
(Columbia seems to want her in Comp Lit;
To wrap up German, she plans to summer home;
Six weeks of classes ought to manage it.)
A snapshot of her, with waves and foam,
Keeps him resigned until the dog days hit.
Sleepless, sweatsoaked nights, afoot with despair.
The fan revolves, thrums and says, "Hang in there."

III.   Meriwether Lewis, to intimates
"Merne." A native of Albemarle County;
Family friend of Jefferson, his trusted
Secretary. The Virginia patrician's dash
And courtesy. Dark hair and eyes, slender,
Graceful in bearing; reflective, a "lover of nature."
Not yet thirty when he took command,
To which he's well suited—except for his temper,
Bouts of depression. Half-orphaned; devoted
To his mother; unmarried. A scholar, a writer.
One can share his delight in the "lark-bunting,"
With its upward-spiraling flight and song; conceive
Why he named rivers "Maria" and "Jefferson,"
Or a Montana crag, "Tower Mountain." And wonder
That his life stopped so short, an ugly end.

William Clark, who answers to "Will," some four
Years older than his dearest friend. A giant—
"Captain Redhead" to that Bird Woman he nicknamed
"Janey." The powerful frontiersman's looselimbed gait,
Water-blue eyes, square jaw. Hair
Knotted behind his head in a firm stump.
An automatic staunchness; cool wits before
Danger; and generosity of affections.
At the close of the expedition he will ask,
And be permitted, to adopt Janey's toddling son—
Baptized "Baptiste," since names create the real.
Merne and Will, their bond as much a period
Tandem as flintlock rifle and powder horn.
Thus Clark, who married late, protested once,
"The friendship of men is the only one that lasts."

IV.   Graceless to mingle honeymoon with class,
       Apartment-hunting, all that our move entailed;
       But soon enough we'd settled into place,
       (Whitman, *Song of the Exposition*) "install'd
       Amid the kitchen ware"—a furnished flat
       Off Riverside Drive. No, *fur*bished: grandiose
       And fraying, formerly salon of, what,
       An 1880s Romanesque château
       Hacked into single and double pieds-à-terre.
       You entered through the bedroom, paused, then stepped
       On grassgreen carpet into a high chamber
       With a big marble fireplace carved in rapt
       Mêlée: coquilles, acanthus, spiral pillars,
       And central triton puck whose branching thighs
       Unscrolled in supple coils to either side.

       Here we unpacked. And made up a true-romance
       Story about our Gotham-Gothic home.
       Yet with your sister Liza's color prints
       Hung on the walls, genteel bordello gloom
       Began to lift. . . . Remember when we sat
       Down to our first real dinner, tall windows
       With leaded lozenge mullions letting late
       September dusk and, sure, some long-stemmed candles
       Play two tones on our table, flickering
       In time with Mozart (K. 622—
       His warmest work, did I agree? Your "theme song.")?
       I do. . . . So topics would arise: Watteau,
       Bergman, the *Sonnets*, a speech of Reverend King.
       And always we knew (knew almost audibly)
       That U.S. fire was tearing through Hanoi.

V.   Thus my baptism in the life as two,
      Gently eroding the loner's dogged truth
      In the brisk weather of love and challenge both.
      The bookshelf came to bother about me less,
      Conceding some could cope without the help
      Of, say, *L'Immoraliste*. In fun ways boss,
      You chose our entertainments, whether a stroll
      Along the Hudson or evenings red and gold
      At State Theater to smile and thrill
      At *Agon, Jewels, Baiser de la Fée.*
      Love was lean as the practice-clothes ballets,
      That is, when not a whispering green gauze,
      Spectral extravaganza, taut silk swell,
      Elan aloft in a luminous mist of sweat—
      Oh pleasure dances best when paired with thought.

      Can you have guessed the gamut of your tastes,
      For you a snap attainment by the way,
      Remade my own (let's hope the lesson lasts)?
      No wish to paint, you had the artist's eye,
      Alert to nuance and color till then blind
      Platonic cavemen never dreamed of. And,
      Praise be nurture, you also knew from cooking
      Since childhood what a civilizer food is.
      Cordon bleu without diplôme, you'd take on
      Gourmet summits not outside Lutèce
      Likely to pose as daily bread; though fuss
      And fanciness came in for scorn as much
      As plain-fare herbs and apples. "Meat and drink!
      Tomorrow we must demonstrate. That plonk
      Will do, but please no Spam." (And, *Notes*, be song.)

VI.   She's grown accustomed, more or less, to living
With a smooth-skinned, at times incandescent, at times
Moody room- and soulmate. His tenderest
Moments please her best; and that playful, skittish
Miming of people, voices, objects, concepts
(Exaggeration, *un*resemblance being
What makes them ring true and funny). Yet
Even though he does better in this line
Than Bert, she wishes a male could ever see
Women as distinct from live-in servants. . . .
But gripes aside, these first fine months begin
To take seductive shape as a dream before
Now scarcely intuited. Why shouldn't they
Bring off the feat and both be lighthouses
As scholars, leaders of the brilliant life?

She sees she's grown a little tired of hip
Habits and politics. Or else they've simply
Been displaced by a steadily increasing
Fascination with her subject: courtly
Love's evolving fortunes in poetry—
Trouvères, *stilnovisti*, Dante, Scève,
Elizabethan sonneteers and playwrights.
And then the countertrend in which Petrarch
Is hustled off the stage to jeers and hisses.
For where do women fit in all of this?
Praise to Dante for writing in a vulgar
Tongue chattels denied Latin could read.
But literary Neoplatonism.
It only threw a stumbling-block the more
In the path of women poets: *Pernette, Louise . . . ?*

VII.   Changes: they argued of and for themselves, as
Hemlines soared to write another chapter
In the red book of hotline revelations,
Airwaves spinning with the London latest
That fans in pea-jackets shook their mare's-nest
Curls to, then dropped, to play a California
Riff on new guitars from some oldtime
Blues or country tune. Ten thousand changes
Past, it's an irretrievable sensation,
The glee that dawned when every day spit out a
New kink, new look, or epoch-making album.
For once behind the times, New York mostly
Served as a clearing-house, eager to welcome
Back what pioneers had left the Village
For good times on Telegraph Avenue.

In fact, Berkeley had folded, so your friends
Announced, who dropped in for an hour that late
November. The truly revolutionary
Core of the Movement had gone to Haight-Ashbury.
A winning spirit of Love and Inner Light
Ignited in San Francisco should spread from there
To the whole world; and stop all wars. We listened,
The mendicant brothers' voices earnest with change
Of heart; and let thoughts play out a tendril
Revery, goldfish swarming into paisleys,
Meshwork mosaic laved downstream the music
Of change. . . . Outside, skies showed silver-gray
Above the sootstained buildings of the city.
And, through small rifts and tears in the cloud ceiling,
Scattered portholes of late, redeeming blue.

VIII.   We marked ourselves off from those who went before,
Those at home in stockades, concocting wars.
Love, having been reinvented, swelled
Into the room, one of the appliances,
To guarantee we shouldn't be possessed.
Enchantment meant to gather while coasting
The skeins of guidelines strewn around to choose
By the magisterial instant, or deduced
From the last nine steps of Temple Unreason,
Top flight of the ever building future.
Risks of casualty crowed to prove
They had no grim designs on righteousness,
Or morning on Crestview Drive. O pioneers,
It was for this you blazed the trail with tears,
That hope might be reborn unceasingly.

Adventure. The word itself is like a tocsin
Sounding the depths of some, of some the life
Of wily outwitting how many decent snares.
We waved blessings over the lightest impulse
As iron self-reliance still commanded.
True, spending an evening alone, or even
For that matter jockeying with a stranger
Craved on cue might leave brashness somewhat
Short on conviction, listless, clearly not
Perpetual; but we could counter to doubting
Voices that this young fresh-air contract
Had innovated; and would spill no blood.
Temptation not to lie is always sore;
Everyone succumbed—once, at dawn to the salute
Of pigeons fired from the stoop to be climbed.

IX.   Telling our story is . . . painful as anything
I've ever done. More painful than. A lapse
Of time so long and I'd assumed, wrongly,
These subjects for the most part would have lost
Their power to hurt. The truth is, now I wish
They hadn't pled their case to me. The wound
Reopens; so clearly was never healed.
What sort of doctoring is it that wounds?
The question raised experimentally,
Either to prove I should renounce or else
Regain the urgent impulse that made me start.
Words and meanings fall into place as though
They were . . . a solid reason to continue,
Some inkling why I want to give them voice—.
I recall, too, periods doing no work:

It all began to turn adversary,
Went cold and brackish. Those who make and are
Made by art soon lose the power of seeing
Very far without it. Their arm, their grace
In the fast stumble and sprain of circumstance.
Linesmiths, who cannot stop a war, relieve
Suffering, change the law, or be televised
Coast to coast, in one small realm can bargain
For peace between words; can make a heavy sentence
Light; resolve a harsh clash in sound
Or sense; and make our kind of English sing.
Is it a pattern, too, for other projects?
We labor until animal magnetism
Draws us into the spirit of the thing;
Come down with a case of hope; and turn the page.

X.   Saint-Gaudens, possibly Hiram Powers
      Might have mustered skill and found which deeds
      To frieze in marble, the hardship dance of hours
      In their long trek upriver to the mountains.
      Sacajawea was, I think, once cast
      In solo bronze, but never the young captains'
      Iconographical self-sacrifice
      Portrayed in the eulogy of adamant.
      Us, the imperfect was our paradise.
      Yet we were always in a way part sculptor,
      Fixing pivotal moments in that Trajan's
      Column, the passage up from phase to phase
      As avatars of higher imaginations—
      Not merely some penciled entries in a journal,
      But records that eternity still plays.

      For those voyages of discovery—
      The slowly unfurling story of Ann and Alfred,
      Or tracking the sources of the great Missouri,
      Or Dante's autobiographical
      And catechistic narrative—all strike
      The keynotes of a cyclic canon, call
      It "Pilgrim Achieves a Soul through Steep Progression
      Toward Revelation," or "The Passage to
      The Garden"—any plot line where a question
      Named Time wins certitude by marrying
      An errand through Space. Though why selected facts
      From private lives, and not some grander thing,
      Should go to build that edifice of late
      Will have to be worked out by questioners
      In other fields. . . . Meanwhile an open gate

XI.   Leads into one distilled from many nights
That winter, sedulous, homey evenings spent
Typing or taking notes for essays; or,
In your case, reading that week's lesser-known
Classic. (You'd joined an informal group of bright
Students meeting Mondays, with cheese and wine,
To discuss *Christabel* or *Modern Love*.)
Yes, let's say that Meredith's obsessive
Jamesian antiromance is what you're bent
Over, frowning intelligently there
Within the hot circle of the tensor light.
I stroll over to you, touch your shoulder
And wait ten counts until you lift a face
Still vaguely fogged with the trance of reading.
"Hm?" you ask; and eyes answer full voice.

No point mentioning again that name
I more and more hear you pronounce (the most
Ambitious of your classmates, they say, plain
But fiendishly gifted, the unofficial chief
Of your cénacle.) You smile and arch your brows
Before turning back to the crabbed sonnet.
I've got it, a hint from Mozart. But you soon
Ask to have it replaced by golden silence. . . .
A silence of a different grain than that
That thins out the air of the room six Mondays
Later, when at some small, stifling hour
It dawns on me you won't be coming in
Tonight. Eventually, you phone. I see,
But can't respond directly to the mixed
Keys—challenge, despair—in your voice. "Goodbye."

XII. All right. If freedom wants to be fulfilled,
      No doubt it needs a household to itself:
      Ann finds a studio closer to school;
      Al, a downtown crashpad in what's being called
      The East Village, matrix of the new
      Mystic-drug-and-social revolution
      (Which can't be launched at uptown rental rates).
      They promise they'll commute to see each other;
      But as for classes, he simply doesn't go.
      No problem. While his right hand dashes off
      A few last papers ("Gautier and Baudelaire")
      The practiced left twirls tight a cigarette
      For impromptu meetings of the *Club*
      Des Haschischins. What the A's received might owe
      To special illumination, does he care?

      He cares about the journey with closed eyes;
      About varieties of mystic thought;
      About perception, its portals flung wide
      To rainwashed color, texture felt in the gut,
      Proliferating symmetries, light figures
      In the optic carpet, magic, music,
      Philosophy at one with the heartbeat,
      With the wild torque of the galaxy, dilate
      Pupil, wheel within wheel. . . . Even the flower
      Tendered by the smiling jeweled devi
      Whose precinct's Tompkins Park encapsulates
      (Its sunbright disc, its radiating petals)
      That first love, the innovating starburst
      Of creation, down to the tiny solar flock;
      To earth; to flesh; and the mind perceiving all.

XIII.   Flaking plaster. Bathtub in the kitchen.
        Closet john, with walls sporting koans
        Inscribed by visitors: "The Buddha is dried
        Dung," above, "The Buddha is *not* . . . etc."
        Mao's Little Red Book hard by
        Growing Up Absurd, The Kama Sutra,
        The Autobiography of Malcolm X.
        Tour of the premises (within a week
        You'd come to see what sort of place I lived in)
        Began with two rooms bald of furniture,
        And then tripped down to the Street. Two doors over,
        Paradise Alley basked in its having once
        Come up for mention in *Howl.* What's more, the guru
        Himself and ponytailed sidekick were often
        To be seen shopping at the corner bodega.

        Not far away, the "Digger's Free Store,"
        For gratis food and clothes. And FILLMORE EAST,
        Where fans could hear the new West Coast imports,
        Or B. B. King, or themselves become a part
        Of the Living Theater's "happening," titled
        Paradise Now. . . . We lounged in the orchestra,
        Not once flinching as the players, stripped
        To cache-sexe and leonine manes, strode down
        The aisles and projected in our faces, "I
        Am not allowed to travel without a passport!
        I'm not allowed to smoke marijuana!"
        "Then disobey," came back the shout from some
        Of us, who brandished notional texts of Thoreau.
        No curtain. But soon we left, pushing outside
        To night, lights, and traffic. We, the living.

XIV.　In due course, I train uptown to check
On how you're coping. What's your news? Oh, nothing.
Well, your colleague's begun to show
His true colors. A bully like them all.
Fresh out, *Sergeant Pepper's Lonely Hearts*
Club Band drops to the turntable, spinning
Rueful fables of constraint and freedom.
And gives a hint of having anticipated
(After earlier successes) the slight
Disappointment we feel. Its jacket features
The stars, in psychedelic Salvation Army
Uniform, gazing down at what might
Be their own grave, bloodred hyacinths
Spelling out the name that launched ten million
Discs, and a raft of famous dead behind.

"The love that's gone so cold and the people . . .
And life flows on within you and without you."
You stretch, begin to do a little housework.
Is this the moment to note again how feeling
Tends to override its simplest settings?
The props, and maybe the actors, too, will seem
To matter less than the high voltage channeled
Through them; so that even here, as you stack
Records and papers, in faded shirt and jeans,
You are all you ever have been, ever.
A votary will need no gilded stage,
No ambrosial music, no holy terrors
To be caught up in a silken spin that makes
The conscript dancer sense his happiest role is
To foot a rough equivalent of The Dance.

XV.   March 26, this 1967.
       A blue and sunny Easter morning. And we
       Converge on Central Park, in Sheep Meadow,
       To pour the crystal vial of our souls
       Into an ocean of young elect gathered
       Here to demonstrate the power of
       Doing whatever pleases you—a new
       Abbey of Thélème, uncloistered, motley, free,
       And billed "The First Central Park Be-In."
       A*L*L*E*N*, bearded, in Krishnamurti whites,
       Strikes a hand-held gong and leads a chant
       Designed to tumble down some towers of
       The hostile Jericho, Amerikka.
       The crowds begin to mill, to shout and run,
       A rainbow wave that breaks across the field. . . .

       And yet and yet and yet: some part of us
       Is not dissolved in the unanimity,
       The anonymity; sees little point
       In swallowing a daily hallucination;
       And flatly disbelieves that Love is all
       It takes to stop a war. Granted *something*
       Must come to replace their moribund régime;
       But sturdy, reasoned, made with but never solely
       Of freedom, pleasure, inwardness and light.
       Besides, who can forget the demon, the guard,
       The graybeard, and the thief in all of us?
       We stroll among much smiling innocence;
       Wonder, and doubt. The nature of a trance is
       To lift and leave a lucid calm in its wake.
       Which finds us turning to go, your hand in mine.

XVI. By Dante's subtle twinnings Purgatory
      (That late-patristic timeclock metaphor he
      Took as the gospel) finds its counterpart
      In Mount Parnassus; and the labor art
      Exacts from journeymen is figured in
      His staggering climb from haplessness and sin
      Up to celestial heights of expertise
      And grace—which leaves him more than skilled to please
      Angel and mortal alike in sacred meter.
      Since Beatrice (though he doesn't meet her
      Till Canto XXX) is saint as much as muse,
      The pilgrim's and the poet's love must fuse.
      If quests lead *to* the father from the son,
      The second of these trinitarian
      Canticles would form the Holy Spirit's bridge

      Between those persons, through the . . . matronage
      Of a stern, loving lady who has discarded
      Flesh for spirit. In the lessons larded
      Throughout the narrative, the pilgrim's taught
      That bondage to base instinct must be fought;
      What his heavenly mistress seems to ask is
      Disincarnation. When she takes to task his
      Earthly amours, it's not mere jealousy,
      No, but prophetic zeal to set him free
      From all the downturned heaviness of nature. . . .
      A lesson for the artist, too? The fate you're
      Born to is only an early rung of that
      Ladder of Vision or pealing Magnificat
      Beyond the Spheres? No doubt. But look, here's sight:
      Which sees the pilgrim still at middle height.

XVII.   The "Summer of Love" left some or all of us
        Behind. Plain living, high thinking had been
        Upscaled for media coverage, retailed
        In new fashions for gypsies—who came in many
        Ages and brackets now, anxiously concerned
        Not to be counted among the blind and old.
        Embarrassing to watch the latecomers
        In expensive rags shake their fists and shout
        Some shiny bit of slang or slogan gleaned
        From a TV special on Flower Children. . . .
        And, as always happens when the parents
        Refuse their allotted role, disgruntled offspring
        Rushed in to fill the vacuum and became
        As best they could, responsible adults.
        (One morning I said "goodbye to all that.")

        I wanted to be with you, this time for good!
        But now, a fellowship to France had dropped
        In my lap. Could we bear a year apart?
        Not again, so therefore both must go.
        Resolved. And just to make it easier,
        We'd better get ourselves a little married.
        The civil ceremony shouldn't hurt
        Too much, you think? (Let's see, a few details
        Need to be brought in here. Our guests: your mother,
        Your twin and *her* Best Man for the supporting
        Roles. We huddled under the Great Seal
        Of New York State and answered questions till
        The clerk pronounced us a legal entity—
        You as uneasy with his certifying
        "Wife" as I with the pompous-sounding "Man.")

XVIII.   Misgivings soon were banished under the spell
         Of Veuve Clicquot in quantity and slices
         Of snowwhite neoclassic ornament.
         Chin-chin go calyxes, the overspill
         Of spindrift comedy making a joke
         Of our no-way resemblance to the pair
         Atop their crumbling ziggurat—the bride
         A touch waxen, the groom seeming to choke
         On cutaway emotions or perhaps
         Too much sweet cake. Some champers, please, for him. . . .
         Then after guests had gone, the magnums emptied,
         Confectionary monument (with gaps)
         Stashed in the fridge, we two subsided on
         The bed. It had all gone as well as could be.
         Now let what vows be made for us as would be.

         An easy dailiness ensued, much more
         The kind of thing we were. Some Shakespeare-In-
         The-Park. A Brandenburg Concerto. Then
         (Decade sacred to the moviegoer)
         Masculin-Féminin, Muriel, Blow-Up,
         Bonnie and Clyde, or some ancient comedy
         Revived and sparkling on the Thalia marquee.
         Always the same film addicts would show up,
         Mirrors of ourselves, the Children of
         The War, in jeans and granny glasses, eyes
         A little red and gently understanding
         From smoke inhaled minutes ago. (A dove,
         Those days, seldom kept to the olive branch.)
         So summer waned. We sipped our sloe-gin fizzes.
         And clucked at the appellation Mr. and Mrs.

XIX.   But let that nonsense be no bar between
       Them. Besides, other prospects are looming near.
       They have their crossing tickets—can that mean
       Two weeks remain to pack a year's supply
       Of clothes and books and household gear? It does.
       Quick as a thumbed comb the days zip by.
       September shoos them up the gangplank, turning
       Back for a final wave. Then all aboard the
       S.S. *United States,* their qualms concerning
       Seagoing travel stowed far below
       Along with steamer trunks. (And their stateroom,
       In paneled iron. With porthole? No.)
       New tablemates remind them this is fun
       A la third class—conviviality!
       And poached flounder. (Just five more days to go.)

       But then it hits. "There's coming up a storm,"
       A steward warns, and—watch it—the Tiller Lounge
       Spins twelve degrees to starboard. Poor form
       To lurch, but how avoid it when a wall
       Lets swing with a wallop and the chairs
       Glide from their places? Spirits start to pall;
       The crowd breaks up. It's bedtime anyway. . . .
       Come queasy dawn, the troops have mal de mer—
       Go above? They stumble up the passageway.
       Heaving bile seas, of snowcapped mountains made.
       The bow plunges into a valley, rears,
       Then dives. Gale winds, rain, brine, the clouds a shade
       Of leaden green. Rivets, bulkheads wince
       And groan. . . . Enough of this. Just hope the ship
       Can take it. The steward says, "I'm afraid

XX. It's staying with us for a couple of days."
His accurate prediction got ground up in
The seesaw hours that labored seamlessly
And outside thought to keep us pounding through
The savage country of the storm. At last,
A night came when nothing seemed to stir
Except our hopes; and just the slightest camber
Rode in the balance. Hand in hand, we strolled
On deck. The moon glided in stillness high
Above a sea of dark aluminum,
Swollen, drugged, asleep. Miles and hundreds
Of miles, and never a light or fall of land
Descried from this battered lamplit chip
(Seen by the moon as a piece of microjewelry)
Whose prow steered, by faith alone, for France.

Le Havre. Bustle of the docks. Baggage,
Customs, the manic boattrain to Paris acrid
With Gauloises. The small change of fact redeemed
By its being paid in francs, and with a smooth
Impersonal politesse, realism that is
But Nature accelerated, the disabused
Quotidian, a *commis-voyageur*
Who appraises and is, warts and all, appraised
Against a background of apple-orchards hurtling
Past. . . . The old becomes ordinary,
A simple stonework farmhouse sending out
Its alley of pollarded trees, a spry curé
On his bicycle—. But we're not eating
Our lunch (which arrives under silver covers).
Eye to eye, in the land where "we" began.

XXI. A low mansard with old-rose papered walls
And window on the rooftops of the Ile
St. Louis—outpost from which we make some calls
To agents willing to find a home for us.
Job done, it's four flights down and cross two bridges
To the Left Bank. Views of the Seine—plus
Shakespeare & Co., in case we feel
Nostalgia for the Lost expatriates.
We do: the cosmopolitan appeal
Of Paris, ageless, calls them still. In fact,
Look-look, a face from home, Ed W.,
Who's saved us one of his few nights here. "I tracked
Down your hotel. How *are* you . . . look just great!"
(We dine and swill in a lamplit cellar bistro.
Stumble through dark streets. Hug. Vow to write.)

Writing. Yes, I'd resolved already to make
An overdue first effort. *What better place
Or freer occasion?* asked a still, small ache
Inside; and when drawn out continued: *Begin
With love and a question. Every novel does.*
Mine I decreed should be as crystalline
As, say, Flaubert, as black and new as Burroughs.
CHAPTER ONE. . . . Long hours. No headway. *Fuck!*
You'd come and try to smooth away the furrows
In my forehead: "Let's *go* somewhere, want to?"
I might, or not, break for a little stroll.
(By then we'd found a furnished studio
Near Place d'Italie, atop the first "gratte-ciel,"
They said, in Paris. Un-French it was, but, cheap.)
"Dear Ed—*Salut.* There's lots of news to tell. . . ."

XXII. When impetus for fiction slowed, I had
My dissertation-sleuthing to pick up.
The topic, "Melville and Camus," would cut
Across two disciplines and chase the dread
Spectre of being less expert than those
Raised in the French tradition. Certain keys,
Moreover, fit appointed locks. I'd thought
For years that Melville's *Moby-Dick* (no doubt
Our greatest quest-romance) would surely have
Readers among new French auteurs. Camus—
A guess I seemed to make by *déjà vu*—
Had borrowed from it in his purgative
Fable *La Peste*. . . ? And when she gave me leave
To catalogue his books, I went to call
On Mme Camus, his careful widow; saw

That *Moby-Dick* and other Melville figured
In his small library. *Et bien*, the proof
Is there, should scholars wish to follow through.
I guess I am, for certain things, a sluggard—
But still perceive the fertile field of, well,
Franco-American cross-cultural
Influences has never fully been
Explored. Beginning with Napoleon,
From whom we bought Louisiana, and
Directly to the present, these two fast-
Thinking and -acting countries always had
Eyes for each other. (Baudelaire retrained
Himself on Poe. Flaubert-Laforgue, through Pound
And Eliot, invented modernism.)
Why not a show, "Paris–New York"? *They did one.*

XXIII.   Bread and wine. Mint tea at the Mosquée.
Chèvre, watercress, escargots—
Just a few of the blandishments I must
Resist in order to recount the always
Less sensual, bonier aspect of life,
Its meaning. . . . Paris though it was, we found
The war for Vietnam would pitch some battles
Here as well. Chagrin over not being
Part of the giant march on Washington
("Lowell and Mailer at the Pentagon")
Subsided when we learned we could still fight
By joining the French *Comités de base.*
Rallies. Demonstrations. Position papers.
Hawking one of the *Militant* weeklies,
I was ordered by French law to decamp.

And muffled my answers so as not to be
Pegged as an "agitating alien," one
Of those many about to be deported.
Heady excitement. And a welcome change
From my humdrum toil in the Reading Room
Of the B.N. So what if committee powwows
Leaned toward arid disquisitions more
Concerned with P.C. theory than the plight
Of Vietnam under the bombs. Better
This peripheral effort than a year
Of helpless silence. *En marche.* Meanwhile, you,
With no official job of work, would read
Ariosto and Spenser for fun and to prepare
For next year's courses. (Patient, wan, you smile
At your tired militant, who waves from the door.)

XXIV.   *Directions Clignancourt, Lilas, Italie—*
We circled round and round the city, now
Taking a bench in Place de Furstemberg,
A kir at the Café Voltaire, a browse
Along Boul' Mich', an amble through Cour de Rohan.
Evenings there were doubles at the Cinémathèque,
The Grapes of Wrath, perhaps, with *Les Enfants*
Du Paradis. (Balletic marvel, appeasing
Realism's scruples with its fable
And the panache of the young French Bohème.
Think, to be Jean-Louis-Pierrot and mime
Pleas so searing to Arletty-Garance—.
Chromatic melancholy, bittersweet as
Paris, its lilac rubato took the reins
Of the G-minor nocturne of Chopin,

Our Rubinstein rendition played and replayed
As the cloudy months devolved into one seamless
Pearlgray year. . . .) Year that included a quick
Hop across the Channel for Christmas in London:
Which had geared up as San Francisco East.
I look back now, bemused to see how much
We kept on the go, drawn like ferrous pollen
To the complex magnetic rose of each
Old enclave of art, no matter how askance
The welcome tendered to young America.
Paris, London, Amsterdam, Vienna,
Venice, Athens: the scroll of central cities
Unreeled and spilled rich plunder for the soul—
Not least a sacred discontent with all
The scarscapes tilting underneath our plane.

XXV.   Its spokes converging on the stapled hub
Of the Etoile, Paris wheeled into place
Below. Another turn, and then Orly.
(How many revolutions since, the one
Step by step preparing then has come
To seem respectable almost, a bookend;
But who in 1968 foresaw it?)
Step one: *l'affaire Langlois*. The founder of
The Cinémathèque was suddenly dismissed.
Sartre, the universitarians,
P.C. intellectuals and all
The filmic world joined forces to protest.
J'accuse's, posters, letters. Finally
Malraux, as Minister of Culture, acted
To reinstate the ineluctable.

Reason the Goddess smiled as left-wing praxis
Took careful note, and all of us bought tickets
For *Potemkin* and *October*. But now
Students here too began to feel they
Possessed a special gift of divination,
Restiveness, challenge, rage, their common fuel.
Targets: Vietnam partitioned by foreign
Fiat. Consumerism's python grip.
The "hospital society," which counted
Almost everyone by now, the poor,
The ghettoized, the sad, the numb, the mad.
Keep Southeast Asia safe at any cost
For Western anomie? The blinded leaders
Knew not what they did and must be helped
Or pushed to see the right; but soon, before

XXVI. The plague had spread past hope of remedy.
Discourse volleyed back and forth between
Nanterre and Place Maubert, *Défense d'afficher*
The first restraint to crumble as the walls
Papered over with grievances and slogans,
The wise and ardent icons, Chairman Mao
And Che Guevara. For the first time in decades
The International assumption rang
True. And here was electric news from home:
Columbia had been taken over, shut
Down by the S.D.S. till further notice.
The gray sandstorm of a wire photo
Coalesced around a teenaged striker,
Feet propped on President Kirk's desk,
Puffing a cigar beneath a Rembrandt portrait.

Not since Berkeley, we thought. . . . But what about
Our friends—teachers, students, who might be caught
Up in the drama? Telephone parleys,
Expensive, curtailed, picked their way over
A minefield of conflicting sympathies.
Which tipped in favor of the protest once
Guards swept down and cleared the buildings, clubbing
Anyone too slow to dodge. For blood
Is still blood, however urgent the theory
That sheds it: I'd read my Camus and Rosa
Luxembourg. But didn't bother citing
Them to the *Comité de base*, whose next
Meeting announced plans for a clash of arms
With *Occident*, an ultra-rightist group.
Our chairman's eye locked with mine, amethyst

XXVII. Glint from his spectacles anticipating
The chill contempt he'd feel for me when I
Voiced some objections fostered by "Bourgeois-
Humanist Conditioning." *Whereas*
A scientific grasp of social process
Should obviate the sentimentalism
Of weeping overmuch for those oppressed
Or killed while history accomplished what
Inexorable purposes it held
In store for the People. Merely incidental
People, I wondered? And whether these committees
Really much cared about the Vietnamese.
Wasn't, instead, the point here to recruit,
Indoctrinate, and train new Party members?
Disguise, deception, doctrinal dressing down—

As techniques banal compared to what torture
And murder I knew had been performed before.
"No, I'm not in favor. I resign."
I walked out, bathed in cold sweat,
On my mettle, furious, my back tingling
Where eyes had drilled in before I closed
The door. . . . How easily this all told itself
To you when I collapsed on our sofa-bed.
The city lights began to wink on
Some twenty stories beneath our window. We
Curled up together, exchanging murmurs with no
Ballast of ideology or spleen.
A thick bat of bread on the sideboard.
Three francs' worth of anemones. A litre
Of *ordinaire*—which it was time to decant.

XXVIII.   News from Nanterre: a crackdown no less brutal
Than Columbia's. And then an echoic
Roar of support from the Quartier Latin.
Students ten thousand vocal marched against
The incarceration of their leaders, state
Repression. The Sorbonne closed its doors.
Shouting matches, harassment, and at last
A pitched battle, which deployed in slow
Motion, a liquid nightmare staged around
Collagist barricades thrown together
From lumber, capsized cars and paving stones.
The C.R.S., black-helmeted, with shields,
Goggles and nightsticks, swarmed from armored trucks,
Advancing through a fusillade of stones.
Protesters, in street clothes, fell down and bled.

Cries. Distant sirens. The faint burn
Of teargas drifted down to the 13ᵉ.
When quiet returned, I stealthily threaded
My way up toward the brooding Panthéon
And rue St. Jacques, wondering whether some new
Education sentimentale would be hatched
From this unrest. The tower of Ste. Geneviève
Said, "Paris repeats herself, true, but the terms
Differ. . . ." A liberated Odéon
Now featured a round-the-clock debate
Open to whoever could make himself heard.
Groups or solos seized the platform, held it
Till hounded down by boos or *Merde!*'s: total
Dissent voiced in a total democracy.
(I still can't get that noise out of my ears.)

XXIX.   As in those movies of the Forties, when
One after one a pouncing wind rips
Pages from the calendar and time
Speeds past like headlines, thus, disoriented,
We walked through the anarchy, with no part
To play, foreign observers who, if they
Mean to act, must do so somewhere else.
Métro and power strikes, the handbill snowstorm!
Lucien Goldmann confronted with his burning
Renault and shouting, *"Oui! C'est bien, c'est bien!"*
The hoarding and the shortages—this
Hurtling armored tank of happenstance
Where human bodies were maimed, real blood spilled,
Could hardly note the anguish of mere extras
Or be affected by minor interventions.

The million-strong national protest march.
DeGaulle's clandestine leave. His plebiscite.
Each newsflash took on a retrospective
Cast, as though unfolding at the remove
Of several decades; as though History
Could only be recorded, never fully
Lived. . . . And life was what we chiefly had
At heart, that paydirt any but the stager
Of self-immolation will, I think, have been
Rooting for, in the smouldering city dump
Of someone's throwaway century.
The lease was up. Time to go back, to struggles
More our own. . . . No, first a pilgrimage
To Italy. To Florence, first, and then
Back to where our passports said was home.

XXX.   Mnemosyne's kisses bring a roseate
       Dawn to the cheek as Beatrice, dressed
       In national colors—white, *fiamma viva,*
       And green—appeared through veils of flowers,
       Primavera botticelliana,
       To Dante. . . . Pausing outside Santa Maria
       Del Carmine, the *Benedictus* still
       Ringing in our ears, we turn our steps
       Along Arno and ponder a mystery
       Miser Time clutches to himself. Rebirth
       Of whom? Sapientia, Caritas, Claritas—
       A host of feminine nouns, ancillary
       To the patriarchal Apostolic Church
       Moved to the place of honor, Hellenic grace
       And strength recaptured from the ruins of Troy.

       Rinascimento's rhyme *Risorgimento*
       Helped Stendhal to his point? That passionate
       Hippolyta in Phrygian cap portrayed
       Bearing Enlightenment's treble standard
       Before a people up in arms could trace
       Her lineage to this holy, chastising
       Muse—that is, assuming militancy
       Left room for largely speculative pursuits.
       The day will come: and Dante, always the surest
       Baedeker for the soul's Great Circle, Dante,
       Whose hand she feels fall slowly away,
       That same Dante attend on her there
       In the topmost green theater of Eden,
       From which Rebellion, weeping tears and clad
       In leaves, once took its solitary way.

XXXI.   Italy, everybody's Arcady:
        Homesick in advance, they leave it, little
        Guessing three years, no more, remain to them;
        And still believe that good things last forever.
        Cognoscenti of declining rapport,
        For you to note divergences that wrought
        Division, causes for rejoicing, some,
        If others, pain. And all of them are past.
        The chronicle (riddled of course with blanks)
        Has a textured corrugation, sweetness,
        And tinge of bruise, say, *Jules et Jim* prepared
        Them for but nothing quite anesthetized.
        Merely in living as and where they live,
        The subjects come to oversee their pathos
        And try to parse the syntax change incurs.

        This twilight preview shouldn't cast, however,
        A shadow on the rest, which held in store
        Some of the sparklingest brio, highest peaks,
        In the whole story. Laughter, pleasure, awe—
        Moments making Memory a diviner
        Gift, I feel now, than pure invention
        (On which in any case the chipped mosaics
        Rely for missing tesserae and patterns).
        It glides upstream the onward course of time,
        Respects most of the structure of creation,
        And gives what's long departed a second chance.
        The loss and dark of intervening years
        Lift then; and let us witness how rebirth—
        Questo rinascimento personale
        E immateriale—can light up an age.

XXXII. Late summer, western Montana. The river
Ascends and narrows toward the Continental
Divide. And Sacajawea, calling, points
To an odd-shaped rock she recognizes
From childhood: close to home, familiar ground.
Lewis draws up short, half-disbelieving.
A shrug, a laugh. The march proceeds, with always
His typecast grumbles from sluggish Chaboneau.
Miles. Nightfall. Campfires. The shrilling darkness.
And when, days later, the little tributary
Shrinks to a musical brook and then a cable
Of water, they come up on a rise to find
A voluble spring, flexing, sunlit crystal,
From which they drink. This is water that will
Run down from here to the Gulf of Mexico.

The first of the expedition's leading aims
Has been accomplished. Reason to continue—
Nor waste time, so over the crest of the rise
And through a gap between two crags. But now
The trail turns downward, west, where range on range
Of snowcapped mountains fade into the distance. . . .
Begin descending the sharp-ridged watershed
Of the giant Continent. A half-mile down
They reach a tumbling brook that tends north
Of west. Another spilling handful of light
To toast this August 12 of 1805.
—Duly recorded, that night, in Lewis's journal.
His first taste, he says, of Columbia waters.
A solid warrant, too, that they might hope,
Oh soon, to reach the great Pacific Ocean.

XXXIII.   It would be hardly truthful if I said
          We boarded the ship without a qualm. The crest
          Of each westward-breaking wave recapped
          Many an intuition one was half
          Willing to let roll back into the deep.
          Distractions, though, were near, in case of need:
          New *Pléïade* Prousts, our bodies, nightly toasts
          To the shade of Bessie Smith, to Chairman Ho.
          And still, I'd gaze for hours at the blue
          Expanse, its shimmer-silver foils, to brood
          Over Columbus and his voyage—not
          How he managed it but *why* he felt the call.
          Riches? Glory? Soon as pronounced, the words
          Are snatched away in the wind. . . . Day four: I turn
          To you, accomplice, *chère âme*. No joking dismissals?

          (Tomorrow, ushered in by tugs and whistles,
          Our right-on-time *United States* will find
          The harbor's open door with, on one hand
          —Gothic and Machine Age linked together—
          The triune Brooklyn Bridge, and on the other,
          Lifting her verdigris torch straight up into
          The arc of molten noon, Miss Liberté.
          To them shall go salutes, loud homage from
          The milling travelers, half-drunk with home
          And looking for convenient icons to thank.)
          For now, let sun, all fire and steamclouds, sink
          Into its golden track; and evening call
          The seaworn pair, who, up for a last stroll
          On deck—he inwardly framing his, she hers—
          Wish on two of the first and brightest stars.

                        ✳ ✳

71

THREE

I. Every desire to be met with glory arises
    From earth as a vine clambers, ramifies.
    If the trellis here for that instinct is

    Three rungs of a letter in upper case,
    I see it now as thronged with leaves and facing
    East to await whatever day will bring.

    When you come to read this, somewhere far
    And someone not your present aspect (starry
    Fondo d'oro icon half made of me),

    Will you stop to ask how feelings that border
    On light hallucination derived or soared
    From what we did and who in fact we were?

    No answer but to cast outside the circle
    Of the self and haltingly concede one's work
    Comes prompted by cues beyond the factual:

    Patterning, some of them; others, preconscious;
    Still others, mythic. The moment has come and gone
    When each detail's commanding impetus

    Was the statistician's, who told "what happened."
    Now, for us, the more than earthly map;
    The strong beam of water; motionless wind;

    The fire that does not char; and silent speech. . . .
    Archer, bending your bow, whose aim is sure,
    Launch from within and yet above the creature

    Conceiving you, O shieldbright stillness
    Hyperbole can never reach yet will
    Always follow westward, always less

    Bound by the downward reel of gravity:
    With strings of fire its trail, *integer vitae*,
75 The comet's at-rest flight regains the sky.

II.   Peacepipe on the banks of the stream Lemhi.
Cameahwait draws at it while, smeared with grease
And facepaint from having embraced one hundred

Warriors, Lewis lets slow-spinning curls
Of smoke wreathe his request for assistance,
His plan to pass through the Shoshone, and reach

The seagoing river. A half-lit gleam in eyes
Seals, or pretends to, the agreement. Adjourned.
In the lodge they offer him (cured skins stretched

Over frame, green branch floor with antelope
Carpet) he sprawls. But now, at the door, his dinner:
A skewered chunk of antelope and—is it

Salmon? Pink-fleshed, steaming. So then the sea
Will not be far. Avid to taste his surmise—and
Ignorant of the chinook's homing instinct.

(First mildly urgent pulls toward a river
Mouth that has just this one taste; the growing
Attraction of swimming far and farther upstream;

Loss of appetite supplanted by hunger
For remembered swerves in a reverse
Path, *this* tributary, then this higher;

And now the onslaught thunder of firebright water,
Huge troughs of bubbled motion, these yearning
Plunges over granite hurdles, slamming up cascades,

One maddened muscle aching forward, there,
To the final spangling birdcalls of a brook,
Gentle flickerings and lulls, a place to wade,

To spawn, one electric spasm, which spills
And lets drain its curling milt. . . . Expire in
76   Delight, three thousand feet above the sea.)

III.   Repatriated. The great rumbling forum
    Gathered us again to its mammoth heart;
    Within a week we'd never been away.

    A new apartment, though, and paid employment
    Marked the change. For reasons to this day still
    Cloudy, it seemed you wouldn't go back to school;

    You'd rather work. Meanwhile, three mornings
    A week I teach my first classes, with some
    Puzzlement at how manifestly little

    The overriding issues of last year matter
    To the wide-eyed ranks of freshman insouciance
    Facing me. Opposed, sure, to the war, or at least

    The draft. What in favor of? Somehow getting by.
    Then, almost without exception, I draw a blank
    With colleagues. An untenured junior

    (I didn't know) should expect to be received
    Like *la cousine Bette.* Cloister of humanists,
    Where were you? Novices seldom famous

    For tolerance, those days I had none really
    For professionals caught like Laocoön
    In the toils of an icecold, deadpan struggle

    For middling spoils and splinters of perquisite.
    (All wonder and praise for that tiny band
    Of friends whose pluck and sense of the ludicrous

    Keep them sane and actually pedagogic
    There where most cannon-fodder succumb
    To the foregone institutional fate.)

    Dogged, unseasoned, I plodded through the term
    With nods and brief rictus for them. Then once
77   Home, a groan and roll of the eyes to you.

IV.   Sunday mornings, stretching into the afternoon,
We would negotiate the day in bed.
Grapefruit, book review, coffee, telephone.

Snowcooled light through open shutters;
Copland from the speakers; always the ground-bass
Knowledge that tomorrow you'd trudge off

To that humdrum office job that meant nothing
At all to you; and I, in turn, to my classes.
Tonight? "Oh, Ed's coming over to read

The draft of a chapter from his novel." (Which,
Urged on by us, he will complete, dedicate
To us, and publish—but that came later.)

Meanwhile, my Paris pages have had the savoir
To find a nesting place in a bottom drawer;
And I've been kicked upstairs, yes, back to poems.

How to begin? Prowling the bookstores
And finding no epigones of Baudelaire,
I wondered whether someone might not still—.

Long since destroyed, a few early trials
Float back now in outline—with their subjects
When so equipped. Wasn't there one about you?

Or about a silence, a distance I felt sometimes
Between us. You were ensconced halfway across
The room, absorbed in reading *The Second Sex.*

The Siamese lately acquired crouched
Next to you, tail flicking. . . . And so on.
Nothing "mystique" in the cat, or of Jeanne Duval

In you. A mentor chosen consciously
Often dries up on the vine. Something else
78   Has presided—homegrown; looser; stranger.

V. A day of hardship delayed, Clark and his party
    Rejoin Lewis. Rushes of reprieve; and special
    Happiness for Janey, on home ground again.

    She breaks into a dance, which all
    Watch and approve. The merged parties
    Begin to stride toward the Shoshone camp,

    A measured chant struck up by the tribesmen,
    Singing until there. Out from the crowds darts
    A woman, who clutches at the returned exile.

    Their recognition scene ensues, its burden
    That these two had been captured, both, the same
    Raid, with one escaped and one lost until today.

    They grip arms, face to face, gaze locked
    To searching gaze. Who has really returned now?
    Then relent: the soul *is* there, still alight. . . .

    Protocol. Clark must be made known to the chief.
    In his tent, built of willow boughs, moccasins
    Come off as all sit on skins of white buffalo.

    Renew the peacepipe. Into the captains' hair
    Tie friendly tokens cut from mother-of-pearl.
    Now summon Janey. Who arrives, is seated—

    Only to leap up again with a raw cry.
    And fling herself on the neck of the ruffled
    Chief. Tears, embrace, excited syllables.

    She draws her blanket over their heads,
    Captains at a loss as the muffled interview
    Is conducted. From the pipe a steady upward

    Streamer of smoke. Then the blanket drops.
    A stammering Sacajawea, unveiled, explains:
79 "This Cameahwait is my only brother."

VI. Midwinter thaw. Abruptly it replays
     Our meeting here three Februaries since.
     Fire and ice, sleepless nights, short days

     Restored, without notice shunted back
     By sunfilled waterdrops spilling from
     Rooftops, clearing streets and gutters. Black

     Branches snowmelt bright in the park stir
     And gauge the air. . . . Indoors again, we'll tug off
     Galoshes, let them drain on newspaper,

     The muddy dregs smear over stricken
     War news headlines. So far, nothing avails,
     Calls to Congressmen, marches. The sickening

     Deployment of violence both here and over there
     Gouges deeper into consciousness,
     Unyielding as a game of solitaire.

     —The backdrop for our youth. Would it leave
     Us unscarred? (Reply withheld until old
     Age comes bearing it, with a wrinkled reprieve. . . .)

     Nearer horizons then: this summer we
     Think of traveling West to visit your mother out
     In Oregon; a longtime wish to see

     Your childhood haunts and friends. Besides, we wanted
     To drive overland, a motive in itself—
     Iowa, Nebraska, Wyoming, the vaunted

     Big Sky, exotic names that preserved some
     Of the Pioneers' sunset splendor. Also,
     Reading and liking *On the Road*, I'd come

     To see its narrator Sal Paradise
     (The Kerouac stand-in) as a late avatar
80   Of Whitman. Perpetual journeys: why not splice

VII. Them onto our free-flowing Interstates?
      Another neat idea already scooped:
      For (this is next June) my scanner focusing

      On the van passing by, the name of its make
      Snapped into the foreground, brash as AM radio:
      Open Road, trim designation of the myth

      That fueled a seemingly inexhaustible
      Stream of internal-combustion self-movers
      Cruising behind, around and ahead of us—a myth

      Well inside our awareness and inwardly
      Rehearsed as rolling Ohioan fields
      Slid along the greased, flexible ribbon

      Of I-80. The last handful of images
      From Philadelphia (our first landfall)
      Thin out like a scrim over the present scene,

      The spire of Independence Hall coinciding
      With the steeple of a Lutheran church,
      Urban brick with the squarecut barns

      Painted brick-red and crisscrossed with chalk-
      White trim. Watertower to silo, antenna
      To windmill, the farms approach, swell,

      And subside as we make steadily westward,
      Just skirting Cleveland and Toledo, herds
      Of us on our ten thousand errands,

      The social contract here a matter of lanes,
      Of life and death (since a heedless or hasty
      Runover from slow to passing could kill how many

      Independently cooperating citizens,
      All mindful that the rule "Drive and let drive"
81   Arises from each one's having his fair destination).

VIII. Lunch break: a wayside diner where the pilgrims,
A dozen twelve-wheeled transports congregate
Under the persimmon-gold SHELL emblem.

We push into the clatter, the forthright
Rancor of frying bacon; sit at a blue
Formica counter before an altar with covered

Pedestal enshrining (on snowflake doily)
Half an angel-food cake, vanilla iced.
Octagonal salt and pepper buttress

A fluted sugar caster with stainless lid.
The waitress marks her hieroglyphs, assumes
The office of cook, celebrant at the greased

Expanse of iron beside her two solemnly
Gleaming coffee urns with steam-pipe fittings.
She incants along with Nashville from the box,

Into which patrons' quarters are slipped.
(The lonesome highway's too long and hard to drive
Without the tremolo and flex of dewy steel

Strings, the stretched-out snap and yodel
Of a whisky baritone, his confidante
Hand-held mike soaking up love, the honey,

The gall, easy as bubbles rise in beer. . . .
Or that one in denim picturing this year's month,
Who waves and grins from a John Deere tractor:

He knows the tune, a former one-eyed jack
In the honky-tonk pack. But that's all past;
The farm fills up his time. And dinner's waiting.)

For us, three more hours in the saddle.
"Thank you!" says the check. We step outside,
82   Polaroids slipped on. Midday. Midwestern light.

IX.   A secondary road in Indiana. Now
       Striped barriers and a black-printed X
       Bring us to a halt. No train. Or—.

       Thunder-delicate depth-charges as the missile
       Rockets into view from the leftward south.
       A ragged smear of magnified trombone. The engine

       Volleys by, and then, bringing up the rear
       In rapidfire parataxis, a running headline—
       N.Y. CENTRAL-LACKAWANNA-B & O-

       SOUTHERN-ATLANTIC COASTLINE-READING-
       PENNSYLVANIA-ROCK ISLAND-ROCK ISLAND-
       GREAT WESTERN-SOUTHERN PACIFIC-SANTA FE-

       GREAT NORTHERN—in mid-sentence is erased
       By the access we drive into, the speed-read
       Cartographic résumé still ringing in our minds,

       So that now, our featureless, wraparound
       Horizon seems unreally quiet. But wait:
       At the vertical, something hangs, oh look, a hawk,

       Stiff-winged as driftwood, floating on updrafts.
       Then tilts and slaloms down a ramp of air,
       Talon-first, for consummation with whatever

       Has strayed too far this time from its burrow.
       Down! Then up again into the sun; and gone. . . .
       And when we reach Chicago (flashing assembly

       Of monuments upthrust to futurity)
       Our first effort is to comprehend the lake:
       An inland sea, with fair-sized breakers. Dayfall clouds

       Compiling colors. The sun lets down its golden pipes
       To drink; and plays a silent toccata of water
  83   And light. Tapped inwardly, but shared companionably.

X. During your turns at the wheel and when I
    Break off reading (Dickinson, it is)
    I find myself looking at you, profile,

    Odd flickers of amusement, the daydream gaze.
    Those distances we have come: a falling away
    From the time that was? Early pyrotechnic

    Cloudburst subsided into complacency,
    Complicity; and we old marrieds after all?
    Plausible. And still no child to bind us fast.

    (You said you didn't want—and Mrs. Sanger knew
    We couldn't afford—one.) Voilà. We hopscotch
    Through a slew of sleep-dispelling topics

    As a redwinged blackbird alongside numbers
    The fenceposts. Fields of sunflowers. Then
    A harp of humming high-tension lines upheld

    By a stately single file of korai, latticework
    Valkyries, hieratic pose and features
    Cubist as the kachina doll's (their cyclic

    Ceremonial a mute channeling of power
    From hydroturbine to relay stations
    Sacred to the cult of Transformation; and

    Thence to devout subscribers, who deep absorbed
    In a TV science program on the natural world
    May recognize the more than metaphoric

    Connection between its myriad electrons
    Stinging that sunflower into center screen
    And Lord Helios himself). But where are we?

    Approaching Rock Island—and the Mississippi.
    Ten minutes to nerve ourselves for the crossing. . . .
84 Now, over the bridge into Iowa and the setting sun.

XI.   This land-between-two-rivers, tornado
Country, our journey's third "I":
Now Iowa City rolls out its lawns, its white

Edwardian gingerbread, the chestnut flowers'
Alpha glowing like torches among the leaves' Omega.
Twilight. A Guest House. As we carried

Luggage up the walk, cardinals in the trees
Played flourishes on sopranino recorders.
A light flicks on from the screened porch. "Come in. . . ."

Morning. On the road again. Plains, barbed wire,
Gray barns, all crowned, gable on gable,
With a lookout cupola. Between two rivers:

As we near the great Missouri, travelers'
Anomie begins to lift with a deepening sense
That headway can be made, even here

Where the track runs arrow-straight a dozen miles. . . .
Council Bluffs, goodbye. Suspension bridge
Into Omaha, a prairie town grown large and steely.

Look around? The Western Heritage Museum,
Against whose wall leans a drifter, in boots,
His Stetson tipped forward over coalblue hair.

Creases, dark eyes, the eagle profile. A glance
Cuts our way as he lifts his pint and swigs.
Nods back when acknowledged; then moves on.

As we next, out across the treeless, houseless plain.
Not since the Atlantic crossing have humans seemed
So negligible, the round earth so vast as in this

Unbounded, existential bleakness. Space,
Distance, solitude: nothing standing between here
85 And the Twister but your hat and your luck.

XII.   Cheyenne to Denver, a roughed-up terrain
Productive of sagebrush, tumbleweed, and stunted
Filling stations. Low cloud ceiling overhangs

As we branch out on an excursion (Boulder,
Then Estes Park). On what other continent would
Wayfarers pass, first, a Dow Chemical plant,

The DENVER MART, and a Pillar of Fire Temple;
Then leave them behind for a sidewinder ascent
Up St. Vrain Canyon to the Medicine Bow Mountains?

The roiling, writhing river careening down
Over shelves and stones, mists, clouds, jaggedly
Grown pines with condor grip on outthrust rock

Faces of the canyon—just as we'd seen them brushed
In ink by Northern Chinese sages seven or so
Centuries ago. A "soul" gestured from every cliff

And tree, all self-known beings foregathered
Into the limitless dissolves of heaven's raincloud.
(And how often we were prompted afterward

To consider that, west of Rockies, landscapes
And flora seem imported from the Orient—
As in fact were their first colonizers,

Whose descendants still seem so much at a loss
Before this latest Occidental overlay.)
Picnic on the mountainside. The idle

Ski installations look forlorn and detract
From the view. Here on this highflown rooftop
With peaks in eight directions, which is more real,

An uninhabited eternity, aloof
And paintable; or the familiar machine-made
86   Works and future scrap of our fun-seeking era?

XIII.   In Santa Fe the constellated night
Whose Dipper swings low as if to douse the desert.
For every star, three cicada voices, a sense

Of the world's orb turning through a mesh
Of sound and starlight. As many low roofs
And white houses as can be made out in darkness

From our hotel balcony represent the town,
Its trustworthy human scale. Close of day,
A day on foot through ochre dust, the bending

Streets of the Barrio de Analco. Timeworn
San Miguel. Arcades of the Governors' Palace.
On brown arms, silver and lumps of turquoise, smoothed

Pace of conduct, deliberate, fated, at one
With the cloudless sky transfixed by a single
Crossbeamed silver sun. Completeness, like the rounded

Snow of adobe. Reticence, like the shadows
In half-seen courtyards. Measure, like the gait
Of the Hopi. Dire foreknowledge, like the lightning

Zigzags of the Navajo blanket. Persistence,
Like the soft green and tufted sagebrush
Invisibly propagated out to the horizon.

Uproar of stars, or, here, *estrellas,* in the deep
Night of a piece with that night stretching up
From Mexico, night our unviolent conquistador,

His legions the stars speeding through space
At archangelic distances, no barriers
Withstanding, even at last the imagination,

Rooted as it must at first always be
In place and time, until these are swept aside
87   Before the onrush of what never began or ends.

XIV.   Late arrival at Flagstaff meant no room
To be found anywhere; until a last flophouse,
"The Pine Inn," admitted to having a bed—

Brass and "musical," it proved, as we climbed in
Under a bare bulb, the filament at lights-out
Triply reprinted on the dark. Stretches, whispers. . . .

Dawn. Dress, grub, then a sunwarm drive through forests,
Half gleefully, half grumblingly anticipating
The inexpressible geology of Grand Canyon.

(Here, I imagine, is the place to reconsider
An issue conceivably not laid to rest
Even by *The Prelude, Childe Harold,* or *The Bridge*—

That is, how much crosscountry observation
A poem can fairly admit. Next to fullness
Of feeling, mere recorded seeing should I view

As a negative, an absence, a gouging out
Accomplished by erosion under the headlong,
Superfluent wish to engrave in stone all

Fleeting colors, textures, and patterns of Nature,
All that is opaque to the imagination?
Description, though, goes deeper than a bleached-out Xerox,

Implicitly dispensing so much pleasure or pain.
And is "red" a color? Do wind-stirred pines "tremble"?
When images *Cover the World* like Williams' paint,

Their phrasing still manifests no loss of connotation
Or desire—which often acts simply to affirm
That earth, for some, is "apparel'd in celestial light.")

So for us that day, there at the origin
Of Bright Angel Trail: staggered, trying then also
To find words that would fall in love with what they saw.

XV. The Snake River's Five Mile Rapids too fierce
To venture upon, captains and crew resign
Themselves to disembark and make a portage.

Then, rest and dinner. A crowd of Shoshones—
Different branch of that nation, not Janey's
Tribe—gather to watch (but only in silence);

Accept rolls of tobacco; then glide away.
Now boats in service, which skim lightly
Over one last stretch leading to the junction—

"As a lover might speed to his sweetheart
On the wedding day"—with the Columbia,
Where, on a point of land at the confluence

A peaceful company await their arrival.
Landfall and greetings. Approach of another chief
Leading a party of two hundred warriors,

Chanting to drumbeats, marching up before
The captains and halting in a half-circle.
A proud display: loose-fitting robes of white elk

And buffalo skins with bright cotton scarves—
Cloth that could only have been obtained
From trading with visitors in seagoing ships.

Can bonds be formed with this tribe?
(The Flatheads, so named from their cosmetic practice
Of shaping the cranium into an acute angle.)

The party is taken to an audience with a sage
More than a century old. And a long time blind:
Seated at the center of the lodge, accustomed

To special deference, this squinting Kuan Yin
Talks affably to the explorers; cackles when
89   An attendant begins to describe their appearance.

XVI.   Cool sunlight on the rippling wheat-colored hills
       Of the Bay environs. Buoyant recollections
       Began to surface for you, anticipation

       Based on two distinct epochs in your life, which
       I struggled to apprehend with some echo of feeling
       (Secretly abashed, however, at your having had

       An existence before "us," the one now being confirmed).
       Of your childhood, not much came back, even though
       We passed your first house as we walked to the beach

       For my long-deferred Pacific encounter—grandeur
       At odds with the moderate combers washing up
       On dirty sand among scraps of newsprint, bottles,

       And dried kelp. At our backs, on the boardwalk,
       A ramshackle funhouse broadcast grotesque
       Tape-loop guffaws, farcical comment, one could feel,

       On the Gold Rush. . . . Fog began to tumble in as if
       To mute the sharp factual glare and make turning
       Away from the moment easy as flagging down a taxi,

       The driver briskly dispatched to Telegraph Hill,
       Which ought to occupy the hour before dinner
       With an overview, from Coit Tower, of the town plus

       As many details as memory could add. Afterward,
       We climbed down a vertical "street," wooden staircase
       And landings overgrown with vines and scarlet fuchsia

       Dripping silver beads in the mist-fine drizzle.
       Houses perched intrepidly on the hillside, each
       Linked to its neighbor by a few xylophone

       Steps up or down, the pale white fog overlaid
       On trees and gables like onionskin (on which
   90 The dreamy child traces the outlines of "El Dorado").

XVII.   Wandering the Mission Churches, jolts of context
         Put me in mind of Dante's tomb in San Francesco
         At Ravenna. And of the jaunty flyweight friar,

         Brother and rhapsodist to all creation,
         The founder of poetry in Italian and forebear
         Of a missionary effort active long after

         These Californian outposts. Now his secular
         Descendants, pilgrims of poverty, swarmed
         All around—tonsure, no, but the patched motley

         And outstretched palm of the mendicant (most
         Working out of Haight-Ashbury, which had sunk
         To normal pre-Love depression). Even Berkeley

         Seemed chastened, half-deserted the day we spent
         Visiting your former turf and friends still extant.
         Revolution had subsided into health foods

         And meditation, a reverent stillness suspended
         Over all, the changed times no longer seeking change.
         And rambles up through the hills almost despecified

         One's sense of place as Everysky drew near
         With clouds easily eternal in the worldwide blue. . . .
         Which darkened, later, in the hotel window. Were we

         Up for Chinese dinner? And a walk through North Beach
         To Fisherman's Wharf (if only to prove you hadn't
         Come home again. . . .) That much readier for tomorrow's

         Glide through Golden Gate into Marin sunlight
         And the road to Oregon (last lap through forests
         Of giant redwood, which, with the bristlecone pines—

         Methuselahs among the brother trees, in fact,
         "The oldest living things on earth"—might stand
    91   As a rare instance of the botanic sublime).

XVIII.   Trail's end on the south bank (today Oregon)
Of the Columbia, a likely distance inland
Where they build a second fort and name it Clatsop

For the tribe who hunt there. A roof, dry bedding, chance
To rest, to smoke and store elk meat, sew buckskin
Breeches for the return. Sacajawea proves skillful

With needle, though subject to indoor tedium;
So that when report comes of a dead whale landlocked
On the shore a day's march away, she asks to join

The party sent out to reconnoiter. Permitted?
Permitted, and with the codicil that Baptiste
May accompany his mother—first by canoe

To the seaside camp and then a trek up steep
Tillamook Head, a narrow hairpin trail with shrubs
For handholds up the slope. More than halfway on,

When the sun drops, they halt, make camp, sup, sleep.
Next morning's final upward scrape, then a vista,
To Clark, "The most pleasing and grandest prospect

My eyes have ever surveyed." With his seeing, then,
The brilliant wind, a sovereign stretch of jagged coast,
Massive waves silenced by distance, the scattered rocks

Of Cape Disappointment one side of Columbia Bay
With, landward, smoke from several villages.
A few miles below, the foundered whale, by now hardly

More than a ribcage stripped by Clatsop of blubber,
A bare framework left behind, with the lines of a ship
(Waiting, say, for someone to make an ark of it.)

They go down to the sea to inspect this remnant.
Curling white foam boils around their moccasins.
92   They walk on blurred mirror images in the wet sand.

XIX.   If the journey's single aim had been to track
         The legendary Northwest Passage, there was none.
         Seamless travel from sea to sea wouldn't run

         Till enterprise had laid down rails and driven
         The golden spike. Numberless ordeals undergone
         Taught the captains well enough no one could simply

         Sail across the continent. Yet, attractive trait,
         They never registered complaint or bitterness;
         But readily found a more chastened content in what

         Proved the case. (A well-grounded No can be valued.)
         Sufficient discovery came up in encounters
         With the hitherto unknown, now faithfully set down:

         Maps and timetables drawn and estimated;
         Unclassified plants and animals gathered, described;
         And a first embassy made to lands and nations

         Unacquainted with the new cultural order.
         However little the doctrine stood among the prime
         Aims of the expedition, still one easily grasps

         Why Manifest Destiny and all it led to followed
         So closely on the heels of the captains' return.
         The first hint already gleamed in Barlow's poem

         Declaimed across a banquet table in Washington:
         Columbus! not so shall thy boundless domain
         Defraud thy brave sons of their right. . . .

         With the same soaring genius thy Lewis ascends
         And gives the proud earth a new zone.
         From Darien to Davis one garden shall bloom

         Where war's weary banners are furl'd,
         And the far scenting breezes that waft its perfume
    93   *Shall settle the storms of the world.*

XX.   Portland. But less than ten days pass before
The road-seasoned pair pack up again and drive off
With your mother and Liza (a darker, smaller twin,

Hair parted in neat Indian style, hands stained
With print-maker's black or sepia) to spend two weeks
In a house at Arch Cape by the northern Pacific.

—Ocean that, real, took the measure of its myth,
Breakers toppling over like columns, brilliantly
Cold, onto long beaches of eggshell sand, the air

Mist-milky in daylight and clearing by evening,
When evergreens collected at the edge of the cliffs
To watch the sun ignite a skywide rose window

Before dropping into upheaval, anarchy,
Flamegold and midnight blue, the roiled unconscious,
Alien but exampling what the human includes.

Night brought the moon and a glow shed like silence
That danced among the rocks out to sea, on shoreward pines,
Tempting us from the screened porch down to the sand,

For ritual star census on the beach—vast galactic
Arch of spray, icy pinpricks less numberable
Than the aggregate mist above or sandgrains below:

Here, for any Einstein ready to think of falling
Upward into a boundless mist of light and time,
Was as much of wonder and terror as minds could know;

Until thought, vaporized by magnitude, burnt out
From keeping pace with the speed of light, pulled back
To earth, its spannable feet and minutes (where a body,

Warm, got by heart, accepts the gestures of formular
Protectiveness, shivering arm around slim waist,
94   As two turn and walk back to the lamplit house).

XXI.   Our hike through Ecola State Forest, the same
        Tillamook Head that, sixteen decades before, a small
        Whale-seeking party had climbed, then without the help

        Of pendulum-swung paths up and up through Douglas
        Fir, salal, hemlock, spruce, where now and again
        We caught seablue vistas through screening branches.

        Sweat drops. Mosquitoes. But by lunchtime we reached
        An unvisited cove and settled on a natural table
        In the craggy shadow of a cliff. Along with sandwiches,

        Napa Valley pinot, and nectarines went the bonus
        Of seeing you in your element, relaxed, tan,
        Nicely filled out with summer-holiday flesh,

        Hair streaming in the wind. . . . Like the comet, headlong
        Through time, I can read it now, if then no similes
        Proposed themselves—no more than the Valéryan truth

        That, say, nectarines, to give pleasure, must be
        Consumed; and likewise for these fleeting fair moments,
        Which tell us to love the rose *because* it fades.

        Mostly the sensation was of time to spare, to burn;
        Even to read about the first troop withdrawals
        From Vietnam, the long, dogged recessional

        That would mount up year after year until, at last,
        The ceasefire proclamation. Disasters, too, are mortal?
        They have their conclusions, however incredible

        To a generation for whom war had become
        Axiomatic, an environ that had fostered and hardened
        Habits of resistance not easily nor soon

        Put aside. Though a familiar love, under new skies,
        Could lull them to sleep for days on end, drowning all
   95   Grievances in the sea's millennial white music.

XXII. Once in town again, I remember that, mornings,
       I'd set myself to write. Small things at first. The "speech"
       In still lifes, a vase holding a rainbow profusion

       From your mother's garden, larkspur, daisies, cosmos
       That *required someone to see and hear them, otherwise,*
       What had been the point of flowering at all?

       Not to respond in kind amounted to withholding
       Fullness of being, casting them into outer darkness. . . .
       However untutored my pen, still it meant to relay

       The spark of life—transmitted here as once before
       To the nerveless, upraised hand of Adam. No corner
       Of the universe but a human impulse could warm it.

       And I debated, that July, whether the moon herself
       Felt the fledgling touch of emissaries Armstrong
       And Aldrin, first to vault beyond the sphere of earth

       And air to that bleak eyrie of glare and midnight
       Cold, the prehistoric lunar dustscape. Its broadcast
       Ghostly image sootblack and silver on our screen

       Pierced deeply into unlikelihood, the twin
       Astronauts in bulky diving attire clumsily
       Planting a phosphorescent flag and sowing

       Friday footprints, extrinsic trail markers wind
       Nor rain for all of time would ever sweep away.
       That night, at moonrise, I stepped outside to look

       For changes in the broad, impartial face. No visible
       Signs of gain or loss; but still some faintest sense
       Of a new accessibility *and* a farther

       Numerical remove now that consciousness
       Had logged the entire mileage—its next task to beam
    96 Back terse communiqués to tell us how things were.

XXIII.   Light garden work with you. Visits to Liza
          Across town at her studio. My first stumbling
          Efforts to learn Greek—two hours each afternoon

          With grammar and notebook out on the sunlit lawn,
          Sweat beading and dropping on the subtle inflections,
          The participial fretwork of that streamlined folk and sage

          Creation, the idiom of Athens. Its algebraic script,
          Its phonemes vaguely Japanese, and mild savor
          Sweet and crisp as apples in themselves gave pleasure

          Long before I could parse a single phrase of Plato.
          When progress was balked, I could turn to other things—
          Leaves of Grass (read here again to let its *atman*

          Mingle with the clear air of the Northwest). Or the artful
          Unrepression of *Homage to Mistress Bradstreet*.
          Or news from New York in letters to us from Ed—

          One of which described a rising activist
          Mood downtown after a police raid on a dance bar
          Named "Stonewall" had, for once effectively,

          Been resisted. (Incident presumably modest
          But which led to ground-breaking consequences
          Over the next years, when more and more the practice

          Of simple affirmation became the norm, even
          For those not used to wearing labels or placards.)
          "Good going," you commented and sat down to answer:

          A narrow channeling of desire was part
          And parcel of the "same patriarchal control
          That tries to keep women powerless and fearful."

          A cresting wave of tenderness for you, and your
          American reflexes—you know, those that say,
      97 "I resist anything more than my own diversity."

XXIV. An expedition in rain-filled mist up Columbia Gorge.
To Olympia; to Astoria; to Mount Hood
And the massively beamed lodge crouched at timberline,

From which we set out to climb through courses of scree,
Alpine flowers, and pale blue air. Earthbound reasons
Left whoever hesitantly approached the seat

Of a demiurgic assembly aloft in snowlight nimbus,
Ancestors of awe at rest around the giant throne,
Their names Distance, Silence, Eon, and Majesty.

Now to look north for the Cascades, eyesight ranging
Up each rocky step as if to some origin and birth;
And, following back the palindrome through which light first

Sought and woke the deep slumbering matrix of life,
Let the soul imagine freely heavenward, tracking
A passage to more than India, launching up outside

This ambit to Elsewhere, a rocklike permanence
Not subsumed in matter, motive of the stars and sun,
A logos previous to speech empowering all by love

And gravity, each solar nexus an aureole
Of sensate fire at fullest cry, at edge of brink,
Brought by consummation to send forth a tendril,

A javelin smelted from the overgoing arc of desire,
Embodying the native impulse to find in harmonic
Alternations a reflective Answerer. First

To last, alone and unable to know, each one invokes
The Other, capable to verify what was or is
To be, as shadowed valleys imply the light-capped mountain.

If from this memory, this referential, now I
Unearth, imagine and transfigure a new radiance,
98 I ought not pull back or temper or forget it.

XXV. Summer slows down, gives notice of annual closure.
      And we propose an end-of-season sendoff party—
      Which might as well celebrate my birthday.

      Someone suggests a theme; and why not *The Remembrance
      Of Things Past?* Rôles grabbed or assigned—you
      As Odette, Liza as Grandmère, old friend Gary

      As Charlus, and me, feebly protesting, as Marcel.
      Your mother, with gentle irony lost on no one,
      Puts on a maid's cap and performs as Françoise.

      Late August light out under beeches and hazels.
      Odette in rose silk and a sable ostrich plume.
      Charlus with diamond stickpin and moleskin gloves

      That match Grandmère's powdered hair and eyebrows.
      Françoise pours out linden tisane for a Marcel
      Hardly paying heed—until he takes a madeleine

      And, absently dipping it, tastes. The hand-held
      Home-movie camera rolls and so do his eyes,
      Shocked with remembrance. (An amazement staged and real:

      For in fact I had drunk that infusion only
      Twice before, in Avignon, and then in Paris.
      From "farther than India or China" refracted tears

      Stung the communicant the joke was on
      As Rhone and Seine rose up and overflowed the banks
      Of elapsed space-time, flooding through our tableau.)

      Memory. A retrospective species of hope
      Whereby one catches the habit of recalling
      A future deep as fiction where *all will have been*

      Well—the sparkling source with which we toast
      Hazards undergone and weathered, the fugitive
   99 Years at home finally in the immaterial.

XXVI.   Five months for the expedition's return, rapid
Months of driving hardship and one exploratory
Parting of ways from the Bitterroot Valley

To the junction of the Yellowstone and Missouri.
Our own trip back covered much of the same ground:
Idaho, Montana, North Dakota, U.S. 2

Calling the travel tune and flexible enough
To allow for day-to-day improvisation,
Digressions north or south to see natural wonders

Or historical reminders. And finally to pass
Through what was once Mandan territory, where
The captains said goodbye to Sacajawea (at least

Until Clark should come back to adopt her son).
A separation effected formally, under the sign
Of reason and necessity, once again at odds

With a sense of symmetry and fittingness.
They could meet and form a party only
Here, under these circumstances, and with

These particular aims in mind. Which fulfilled,
No plausible story crystallized to keep
Them in company, however warm their affections.

Captain Redhead and then his partner make
Their farewells as she stands by the threshold
Of her hut, little Baptiste clinging to her skirts.

She sees them turn and go, preceded by their long
Sunset shadows; pause at the top of a hill
And turn to wave, turn, and then sink out of sight. . . .

(The ties of myth and memory connect them still,
Strong as cable, invisible as *caritas,*
100   This three-figured emblem outside history.)

XXVII.   *Les vrais paradis sont les paradis qu'on a*
          Perdus—his meaning, I think, that he could be content
          Only with what was *not there*, provided he found it

          Again, this time a psychic essence within himself. . . .
          My subject is our *union*; which was close even
          At the conclusion—no less painful for all that

          We used the term "amicable." For a long time
          Separate paths had summoned us, a quiet past-tenseness
          Already suffusing our sense of what our couple was,

          When the moment came to make things formal.
          The last two years passed reflexively, you now teaching,
          Marking papers, meeting with your women's group,

          I with no business anchor in the world, nothing
          But a dutiful application to housework and
          A passion for poetry based on few other warrants.

          Then, having struggled to say the right farewells,
          And not long after seen you snapped up by someone else
          (Your new Victor, whom I judged suitable, as you did

          My new Walter); having, by luck, mother wit,
          Hard work, close scrapes, and the patient guidance of friends,
          Come through, I can number myself among the fools

          Who persisted in their folly—long enough
          Now to recommend a less contrary approach to others
          Thinking perhaps to venture something similar.

          Yes, but advice. Would I have listened then? No more,
          I guess, than those who crossed the Atlantic, forsaking
          All, to rebuild Eden in waste wilderness;

          No more than the captains told in advance what dangers
          Faced them; or Dante, given a brief foretaste
    101   Of his pilgrimage back to the lost Beatrice.

XXVIII. Is it useful to ask whether a written text
Restores the best of love or time gone astray?
What's lost, obviously, is really lost; at least for me,

The touch of paper no more welcome to my hand
Than bark to Apollo's as his yearned toward Daphne.
(Once, in Rome, we saw Bernini miraculously

Make the flesh-and-blood god catch hold of her waist
As her fine toes put down living rootlets, fingers
And hair breaking free into evergreen leafage.)

Print, page, nor book is what the authors love.
If they write, the dream of composition, when it descends,
Comes as their compensation—you could say redemption,

That is, as long as the process continues. Do we
Explain it? Or prod the stroking sleepswimmer
And remind him of his duty to wake up and drown,

There in the general shipwreck where vigilance
Has no recourse from that last terrible meeting
Of eyes, before the dark wave rises and divides?

Much like the fast-approaching farewell experience
Teaches me to foresee: soon this writing comes
To its end, conclusion of the trance, the search,

The discovery; and saying the last word. But
Isn't there more, a resonance still to be added?
You know, *your* account rendered of what you find here.

Of course, all the time it's been present to me
That you were the Ideal, the Gentle Reader,
Abler than myself to freely interpret these pages—

Which need not remain "material." Gathered up
Into feeling, read, as now, through a pane of living
102   Water, the letters stir, tremble, dissolve and vanish.

XXIX. Like the jet of a fountain sped from underground
       High in the air with inexhaustible élan
       Consciousness upraises that constantly changing

       Flower flown aloft on the stem of deferred
       Desire, the instinct to let manifest all one
       Is not from within the bounded sphere of self.

       Anima, dancer, indeterminate, the spout
       Of musical light, upstreaming liquid crystal
       Capable to embody ten thousand forms,

       Be called Muse, desirable, potential
       Connectivity of the mosaic of sense and thought,
       Matter transformed by metaphor, love's auspex.

       What part of the patient, always to be renewed
       Labor of becoming mortal takes the office
       Of making you known and seen and audible?

       Or as with China's "male-female" universal,
       Interlocking complements: do you inhabit
       That pivot-point of starlight in the bowed head

       Of its black larva—male principle,
       Warrior, father, word and reasoned structure
       To which you lend another fluent nature?

       Abundant happenstance for a time let converge
       A psychic, finally transpersonal source
       Of energy and an actual, fleshed identity;

       So that this moving image increased, came to rest
       In gentle ascendancy, favored symbolon,
       Sharer instanced now not ever to depart or vanish.

       —To whom I can assign a human face and touch;
       And whose voice I hear, the glancing plash
   103 Of speech, silver fountainhead, these, your words:

XXX.   "You say you hear me speak and when you do
        From everywhere meaning comes riding in—mine,
        In your invention—addressed, in any case, to you.

        Maybe we are still much as we were then.
        Remember how, the laundry done, we'd take
        A clean, still-warm sheet? And clasping the corners

        Advance until our foreheads almost met,
        Join hands, let go, and back away again;
        Then halve the rectangle and both step forward

        To meet again, perhaps this time to kiss; and part
        With one left behind to make a final fold,
        The soft octavo volume safely shelved. . . .

        It's something like the way our paths meet, yes?
        Diverge, converge again, here in this place,
        This summer arbor with criss-cross lattice walls

        And open windows. My sense is that high summer
        (Twenty years now) confirms these reunions,
        The equinox having ascended through May

        To that white zenith that sends down its light
        Like tongues of branching fire enkindling all
        Living creatures to voice or unfurl an answer.

        Mine was always a fairly modest refrain,
        Opposed to cruelty, pretension, dullness;
        In favor of pleasure, play, love without fanfare.

        Starting from there, can we look for something else?
        My idea's to find, with your endorsement,
        Language you might not readily discover,

        To serve as *vale et salve* at the peak
        Where you are now concluding. Is it *d'accord?*
104   Then take—and speak—dear friend, these final folds:

XXXI.   'We keep coming back here to each other,
        And coming back for as long as we like.
        A swallowtail poised above its iris,

        Mars in peaceful conjunction with Venus,
        The comet beaconed from the depths of space
        To ride in highest heaven to the sun,

        Its burning destiny and center, where
        That light not changed by anything it shines
        Upon brings home a life-lease of motion.

        The master-light, the fountain light that sends
        Its messenger with a live coal for me
        To kiss, and be burned and forever set

        Apart, on fire with purpose and a speech
        Foreign almost to all but the nearest
        Senses: rather than answer it I am

        Answered, as this flooding certitude tells
        Me and overflows so that the lowest
        Object, least receptive impulse catches

        Light and is permitted, altogether
        Welcomed, loved, then gathered back at last
        Into the slow diamond of the river

        That first sent it forth. And what is
        Earth but the shadow of another sphere?
        We practiced our memories here and learned

        To harvest a future not ruled by crops and years—
        So much like this hillside grown up in grass,
        With breeze-borne sun, fragrance of earth, of grass,

        Of flowers, the rose-pink and white apple,
        The white rush of a stream hidden nearby,
105   Love's new contentment changing forever.

XXXII.   What hid you? Object that would find the verb
         Able to assimilate its subject,
         The metaphor sometimes traveling in reverse

         So that you belonged also to shadows,
         Uncertainty connecting eye to sight.
         The sun would set, stubbled fields lie fallow,

         The darkness left to find its way alone,
         Origins of love and work beclouded—
         But now the epoch passed and up rose dawn.

         You were nothing if not various.
         The stem becomes the stem by differing
         From its rootstock nor the flower less

         From stem and leaf, contrasting to exist;
         And contracting till it can no more and breaks,
         The seeds of change scattering where they must.

         As seasons come and go like death and sleep,
         The dream of reason wakes to find itself
         In prison; sleeps again; then takes ship

         To other skies, and lends the stars new fires.
         In darkness is forgiveness, no grievance harbored,
         And morning light is prized when it appears.

         Then the red sea closed behind them: here
         Foundations of the city might one day
         Be set in stone, the pillars rise, and there

         Be heard again the rescued psalm of praise.
         In winter, in thick darkness, in the black earth,
         This spring still waited elsewhere for their eyes.

         The great pendulum of earth again
         Swings on its cord of love, revolves, returns,
    106 And calls the sun its star of origin.

XXXIII.   *I am who fulfilled and speak these things, even*
In spirit. And I will always be wherever I am
Heard and known as I am, the last mystery

To come, indivisible, white sunburst
Of numberless stars, victory and comfort,
A lightning certitude, still image of the soul.

Read in the book of life: another race has been
And palms are won; but I will make all things new,
New heavens and earth, sphere within sphere, the power

Given in a true song, its arching wings on fire.
For what it has loved, others will love, impassioned
Remnant whose earth dances with abundance

And the burning summons speaks all names in praise.
The blossoming apple is the Tree of Heaven,
Music the living paradigm of that concord

Which took the part of love in the first ordering.
Now an antiphon with instruments of silence
Notes all things that are made in heaven, petal

And star, perpetual salutation inscribed
In the soaring of the eagle, radiance of this temple
Of fire crowning the young watergold domain,

Inception here at journey's end, the former sunset
Land restored to light, where all build in common
Ecstasy a city raised up in trees and flowers.

This storm of fire, these rainbow tears that make
You stammer, this sweetness intricate through every limb
Witness now what will not be written nor ever said:

. . . .
. . . .
. . . .

*   *   *